Quest for Black Gold

QUEST FOR BLACK GOLD

JEANNE ROBINSON

AVALON BOOKS
THOMAS BOUREGY AND COMPANY, INC.
401 LAFAYETTE STREET
NEW YORK, NEW YORK 10003

PRINTED IN THE UNITED STATES OF AMERICA
BY HADDON CRAFTSMEN, SCRANTON, PENNSYLVANIA

To the one who provided the inspiration

Chapter One

"**N**o women," the job recruiter said bluntly.

"What?" Sarah could hardly believe that she'd heard him correctly.

"No women," he repeated. "They're not welcome at MacDonald Oil."

Sarah was amused. "What happened to equal opportunity regardless of sex?"

He smiled unpleasantly. "You know what happened to it. Not enough states were willing to ratify the amendment."

Sarah felt as if she were talking to a child. "The amendment was only symbolic, Mr. Smithfield. Rights are still protected—"

"So sue us, sweetie." He looked so smug, she could have hit him. "We'd get around any legal problems by hiring you, all right, but we'd keep you onshore, pushing papers. There's no way you'll be wearing a hard hat on a rig with Mac-Donald Oil."

Shortly afterward, the interview over, Sarah stormed out of the hotel and gulped the stale city air. She had three more interviews scheduled for this afternoon, and she knew that she was in no mood to go through with them. Perhaps it was silly, anyway, changing jobs at this stage of her career. Certainly her opportunities at National Petroleum were unlimited. She supervised a group of five and was due for another promotion soon, but that restless feeling had persisted for several months now. She would have attended the New York meeting of the American Institute of Petroleum Engineers in any case, since it was practically in her backyard, but she had been particularly looking forward to it as a perfect opportunity to explore some other possibilities.

She took several more deep breaths, wrinkling her narrow, sculptured nose in distaste. She was sick of New York and its neighboring suburbs. She braced herself and went back into the convention center for her remaining interviews.

The sleek sports car maneuvered in and out of the fast-moving turnpike traffic with ease, though Sarah's mind was not on her driving. All she could think of was that disgusting man who had conducted the interview for MacDonald Oil. She thought back over the final stages of their conversation.

"Why no women?" she had asked.

He ran his hand through his thinning hair.

"Boss doesn't like 'em," he said almost apologetically. "That is," he amended, "he doesn't like them in the field. Likes them in his arms well enough." He leered at her. "Doesn't mind them around the onshore office, either—if they're doing women's work and if they're decorative. But you don't fit his requirements on that basis, either."

Sarah had blushed, trying not to glance down at her conservative outfit. Her long blond hair was swept up into a sleek twist. To the casual onlooker, her large gray eyes appeared devoid of makeup. Her pale gray wool suit, white ruffled blouse, and patent-leather sling-backed pumps had been carefully chosen for a day of meetings and interviews—not with the thought in mind of impressing either this unbelievably chauvinistic creature or his boss with her irresistible feminine charms.

He closed his book, obviously in dismissal. "Try Exxon, Miss Armstrong," he'd said. "They've got a good reputation for hiring minorities."

Sarah threw off the memories of that interview and began to unwind as she spotted the tall towers of Harmon Cove in the distance. She chuckled as she imagined relating the events of the day to her roommate, Barbara. The other interviews had, oddly enough, gone very well, and MacDonald Oil now seemed like merely an amusing incident to relate over dinner. Barbara would find it hilarious; her law firm had handled several class-action suits over far less overt discrimination cases than this one!

By the time she had fought the heavy traffic and managed to steer the little car into the proper lane at the turnpike exit, Sarah was in quite a good mood. She was humming as she strolled past the exercise room and the sauna and down the hall to the elevator. She hung up her coat as she entered her apartment and walked out to the balcony, mesmerized as ever by the sweeping view of the New York skyline. Why, she wondered, had she even considered leaving? This was the area in which she'd grown up; this was home. The difference was that now she had the money to enjoy it in a way that she'd never dreamed of during the difficult years of working her way through college.

The lights of the city were just blinking on. She should have stayed for the evening, she told herself. Dinner and a play would have taken away the bad taste of that interview. Perhaps tomorrow. . . . The convention would be continuing throughout the week.

She turned as Barbara came in. "Barbara," she blurted, "just wait till I tell you about the

impossible man who interviewed me today!"
She proceeded to recount everything.

Barbara took the incident far more seriously
than Sarah did. "It's blatantly illegal," she
fumed. "We could win that suit in a minute!"

"But, Barbara," Sarah protested, "I don't
want the stupid job. It was never very high on
my list, anyway. Can you imagine me in Galveston? On an oil rig? I'm a New Yorker. They
don't transplant very easily, especially to the
South. A Southern belle I'm not."

Barbara was still seething. "It's not that I'm
trying to get rid of you, Sarah, but I think that
you should file suit. Companies shouldn't be
allowed to get away with things like that."

Sarah strolled out the open French doors to
the balcony. "I don't even know what made me
sign up for the interview," she sighed. "I've
never had any field experience; I've been a
pencil-and-paper petroleum engineer since the
day I graduated."

"Maybe that's the reason," Barbara said.

"What?"

"Maybe that's the reason. Maybe you feel
that you're missing something. Remember that
TV commercial a couple of years back? The
one with the gal in the hard hat and coveralls
who undergoes such an amazing transforma-
tion after work when she sheds her outfit and
shakes her hair loose? Maybe it really made an

impression on you. Maybe you city chicks just have to see for yourself what living on the frontier is all about."

Sarah thought about that for a minute.

"Hey," Barbara said, "I wasn't serious. I do think that you should sue MacDonald Oil—and I know that my company will be happy to take the case—but, frankly, I think you'd be crazy to quit your job with National Petroleum. There's nothing wrong with a good desk job; it leaves you filled with energy for dancing every night. And despite the image projected by that commercial, that gal must be dirty and sweaty at the end of that day in the field."

Sarah told herself again how lucky she was as she drove in to work on Monday morning, but the smog hung over the Jersey turnpike. Little patches of unmelted snow lay along the side, filthy with grime. And even the smog couldn't quite hide the belching smokestacks or mask the odor of petroleum cracking and plastics manufacturing. National Petroleum was one of the worst offenders; the flames from its burning vent gases lit up the sky for miles around.

She tried to keep her mind on her work. Her current assignment was an interesting one, an economic study of the various methods that had been proposed for extracting oil from shale. She was annoyed by the persistent image of the girl from the TV commercial, shaking her hair as she removed her hard hat at the end of the day. It was a romantic image, but Sarah prided herself on being a realist.

Barbara confronted her again after work. "I talked to Mr. Johnson today, and he says that there's no doubt that you could win a suit against MacDonald Oil, even though the account of the interview would be just your word against the interviewer's."

Sarah turned to her roommate in exasperation. "Great! And then what? Off to Galveston on the oil rig?" She replayed Barbara's arguments back to her. "I've got a good life here, Barbara. We've got a lot of friends, a nice apartment . . . we're close enough to the city to go in for plays and concerts. . . ."

"I'm not saying that you should *take* the job, Sarah. But somebody needs to teach that company a lesson. It wouldn't take very much of your time. Chances are it wouldn't even go to court. But if you don't protest, they'll just keep on discriminating against women. You may not really want the job, but some other woman might. We're all in this together, you know. The gains that each of us makes helps all of us. . . ."

"Oh, all right, Barbara. You can climb down off the soapbox. I'll file suit against MacDonald. I'm not sure whether it's to fight the good fight for all oppressed women or just to please you, but I'll do it."

Sarah filed her deposition with Barbara, and then promptly forgot all about MacDonald Oil—and, despite a couple of interesting offers, forgot about the other companies with whom she had interviewed at the convention as well. The restless feeling had disappeared as gradually and as unnoticed as it had appeared, and by the time the nibbles started materializing from her convention interviews, she was again content and enjoying her work and her social life.

Her salary was higher than she had ever thought possible. Oh, she had known what figures were discussed, even when she first chose her college major. But the figures weren't *real;* she hadn't been able to translate them into purchasing power. Now she was living with the reality. Her college loans had been paid back on schedule. The monthly payments on the condo and the new sports car did take a large chunk of her paycheck, but there seemed to be plenty left over.

She bought a new dress for nearly every party, ate out frequently, went to concerts and the theater whenever she liked. She had taken a midwinter cruise to the Virgin Islands, had flown to Boston for a long weekend to visit a college roommate, and had started a modest investment program.

Sarah mentally thanked her high-school math teachers again for encouraging her talents. By the time she was ready to think about choosing a profession, the wooing of women into fields once dominated by men was in full swing. She had never had the feeling that any field was closed to her—not until that interview with MacDonald Oil.

Oh, she had encountered some teasing at the beginning of her college years; her classmates claimed that she was too tiny to reach half of the valves in their first engineering lab and not husky enough to turn them, anyway. But it wasn't long before she convinced them that she could hold her own, and the teasing was replaced with respect.

Not that she wasn't feminine. The gray eyes were smoky rather than icy, the naturally ash-blond hair was allowed to hang loose unless she was in a lab or in the field, and the whole was wrapped in a slim but curvaceous package that stood just under five-feet-two. Several of her classmates, and a couple of her professors, had tried hard to get her to respond to their advances.

Sarah wasn't made of ice; she was just filled with determination. Falling in love had to wait. She had been too busy. She had worked twenty hours a week tutoring in the math lab. That, plus the demanding engineering curriculum, hadn't left much time for dating or partying. Just as well, she had rationalized. Falling in love led to marriage, and marriage during college hadn't fit in with her plans.

She sat on the balcony, looking out at the city across the river. The dirt and grime couldn't be seen from here. Now, she supposed, she was ready for marriage—except that the right man hadn't come along. Of course, there was no hurry. She was only twenty-five. Anytime within the next five years would be just fine. She would wait until she was sure that she'd found exactly the right person. She would be desperately in love, of course— though how she would recognize that feeling was not yet clear to her—but not too blinded to fail to check out similarity of background, agreement on her career, consensus on children—not more than two, and not until she was well established professionally. . . .

Barbara came in with the mail. Sarah glanced at it casually, then did a double take. There was a letter from MacDonald Oil. She opened it hesitantly. It read:

Dear Ms. Armstrong,
    On the advice of our lawyers, we are prepared to offer you a field position with our

company, MacDonald Oil, on location in Galveston, Texas. Your position would be assistant supervisor for the start-up of our nearly completed deep-water drilling rig, which lies just beyond the continental shelf. The base salary per annum for a three-year contract would be $55,000. The enclosed pamphlet describes our fringe benefits.

You would be expected to assume your duties by July 1st. Temporary living accommodations will be arranged. Please inform us of your decision by May 1.

It was signed, *Ian MacDonald, President, MacDonald Oil.*

Sarah turned stricken eyes to Barbara. "Fifty-five thousand dollars!"

"You're making forty now," her roommate countered, "and you're due for a promotion and a fat raise in another few months. You already have more money than you know what to do with! Besides, that company is run by chauvinist pigs."

Sarah laughed. "You're right. It was just tempting for a minute. I guess that comes from having to work so hard to come up with enough money for college. But aside from the money, it would be exciting to be part of the start-up of a new rig. And deep-water! That's the most important new innovation in drilling. I could really learn a lot. . . ."

Barbara was beginning to look worried. "Hey, wait. You never said that you might seriously be interested! I wouldn't have encouraged you if I'd thought I might lose a roommate. You've got friends here. . . ."

Sarah smiled, and Barbara relaxed. "I'm not going to take it, Barbara. I'm enjoying my job, and you're right—I've got everything here that I need to make me happy. It's just nice to know that I forced them to come through."

That should have been the end of it, but it wasn't. Every day Sarah took out the letter and read it again. Every day she thought of the experience she would gain by being part of the start-up team for the proposed plant. She was pleased with herself for forcing the company to extend an offer to a woman. Could she back out now? After all, the battle was only half won.

"I'm going to take the job," she announced to Barbara. The arguments began again, but this time Sarah had thought it through. "Come visit me on your vacation," she said and wired MacDonald Oil with her acceptance.

Stupid! Sarah thought as she drove the sleek sports car to Texas. *I should at least have requested another interview. But then they would have found some new excuse for not hiring me. At least now I've got them where I want them . . . or do they have me where they want me?*

Stupid! she thought again as she finally crossed the Texas border. *I'm not even a feminist—not really. This isn't my battle. I don't care whether Ian MacDonald likes women in the field or women in his arms.*

Stupid! she thought as she crossed the causeway to Galveston Island. She was happy that her car was air-conditioned. She had stopped for lunch in Houston and nearly passed out from the humid wave of heat that hit her when she stepped out of the car.

She maneuvered the sleek car through downtown Galveston. She hadn't realized that it was such a sizable city. She had certainly been remiss in her research before deciding to take this job, she reflected ruefully. She had been used to heavy traffic in the North, but she had thought that one of the few advantages of moving to the Sunbelt would be escape from the congestion. And this wasn't even rush-hour traffic! At least the streets were numbered sensibly, and it wasn't long before she pulled into the parking lot of the onshore office of MacDonald Oil.

Sarah sat in the car for a few minutes, dreading the confrontation that was bound to be in store. She hated to step out into the oppressive heat. She glanced at herself in the rearview mirror, noted that her makeup could use a touch-up, then resolutely decided that she wasn't going to waste any time or effort making herself attractive for Ian MacDonald.

She marched up the stairs and into the building, suddenly conscious of the fact that here, unlike Houston, the heat was moderated by the breeze coming in off the Gulf. It was still hot, but not unbearable.

The receptionist was a sultry blonde, a stereotype of what Smithfield might have meant when he said that the only women at MacDonald Oil were decorative and doing women's work. "Yes?" she said languidly as Sarah walked in.

"I'm Sarah Armstrong. Mr. MacDonald is expecting me."

The receptionist smiled warmly. "Oh—the new engineer. I expected you to look . . . oh, I don't know . . . more manly. I'm Melanie." She turned toward the intercom, then paused. "Do you prefer to be called Miss Armstrong or *Mizz* Armstrong?"

Sarah debated for an instant. *Oh, well, what the heck?* she thought. They already had her pegged as an ardent feminist, anyway. She smiled sweetly at Melanie. "To the boss, *Ms.* Armstrong. But I'd like you to call me Sarah."

Melanie laughed and pressed the intercom. "Ian," she said in a seductive Southern drawl, *"Mizz* Armstrong is here."

Sarah had been picturing Ian MacDonald as a middle-aged, cranky Scot. Her eyes opened wide as she got her first glimpse of her new employer. Ian MacDonald couldn't be much over thirty years old. He was tall and rugged looking, with sandy hair worn just a bit too long to be stylish. He didn't fit her picture of a company president, either; he was wearing jeans, cowboy boots, and a work shirt, and had a tan that he hadn't acquired by sitting behind a desk. When he opened his mouth, the last of her preconceived notions was dispelled—the accent was pure Texan.

His greeting was not calculated to put her at her ease. "You've cost me a lot of money!"

Sarah turned on her heel and headed for the door. Enough was enough.

"Wait." The order carried with it an authority that was not to be denied. "You got yourself into this—now don't buck and run as soon as the going gets tough."

It was hard to believe, but Sarah thought she detected a ghost of a smile. "Mr. MacDonald," she said coolly, "I have no intention of being harassed. I'm perfectly capable of filing another suit. I'm also perfectly capable of admitting that I've made a mistake. Shall we end it right now?"

He looked at her appraisingly. "Shucks, no. At least give me a chance to see what I got stuck with. Good glory, you're not even *big* enough to be an engineer!" His glance traveled over her appraisingly. "I hope you won't be dressing that way on the rig."

Well, Sarah thought, her beautifully tailored shirtwaist dress had certainly not impressed her new employer. "I know what an offshore rig is like, Mr. MacDonald. I assure you that I'll be dressed in coveralls and hard hat like the rest of the crew."

He grunted. "I'm sure sorry I got into this. If old Bob Smithfield hadn't goaded you at that interview, you probably wouldn't even have noticed if we hadn't made an offer."

Sarah smiled maliciously. That was certainly true.

"I can just imagine what he said. He won't be doing any more interviewing, by the way. I'd like to have fired him, but he's an old friend of my father's."

Sarah looked up at him with new hope, but it was shattered instantly.

"Smithfield was right enough that women aren't wanted here. The men, especially the old-timers, think that a woman on a rig is bad luck. My father, who owns the company, thinks so too. Never mind what I think about that old superstition. What I *know* is that a nervous crew is bad news—and that if anything goes wrong with the start-up of this baby, I'll find myself transferred to one of our fields in the wilds of Oklahoma."

Sarah was trying hard to take it all in. She had filed a lawsuit—and won—thinking that she was being discriminated against because of her sex. Was an honest attempt to avoid a potentially dangerous situation really discrimination? She wasn't sure.

"Well, you're here now. With a three-year contract. I suppose we may as well make the best of it. Your former employer tells me that you're a good man—so to speak—so I expect I'll get my money's worth, anyway."

Sarah brightened a little. At least this dreaded interview was nearly over. He hadn't quite erased from her mind the image that had been planted by the obnoxious Bob Smithfield. Ian MacDonald didn't want her here, for whatever reason, but there was no reason why she need ever see him again—company presidents didn't spend their time on offshore drilling rigs, especially company presidents who happened to be related to the owner. She was sure that the men would soon see that she was no jinx.

She tried to sound enthusiastic about the

new job. "I'm looking forward to starting work, Mr. MacDonald. Deep-water drilling will be a new experience. When will I be able to get out to the rig?"

"Tomorrow morning. I'll pick you up at your hotel at seven. The day shift starts at eight, and the rig's a fair ways out."

"Surely there's no need for you to go out with me. Perhaps one of the crew or the supervisor—"

He did grin then, a big, broad grin that would have made him devastatingly attractive had it not been for the hint of steel in his pale blue eyes. "Why, Mizz Armstrong, hasn't anyone told you? *I'm* the supervisor."

Sarah's knees felt shaky. He was to be her boss—her immediate supervisor. She would be working with him all day, every day. This was certainly more than she'd bargained for.

He looked as if he were enjoying her discomfort. "What's the matter, Sarah? Afraid I'll make you suffer on the job in retaliation for the grief you've given me? Don't worry. I can't afford to carry my personal feelings to work with me. An oil rig is dangerous enough without having any antagonism between workers. I promise to forget that you're a female during working hours—and I suggest that you do the same. And if we're really lucky, eventually the crew will forget it too."

Sarah blushed. He spotted that and made it worse by saying, "And if you're wondering about *after* working hours, don't worry about that, either. I don't go out with members of my crew."

He pushed the intercom button, and Melanie sauntered in. "Melanie," he said, "I've booked Sarah at the Beachfront Motel for an indefinite stay. Please give her directions. You might also discuss with her some of the more permanent housing possibilities and set her up with one of the agents that handles both sales and rentals."

He extended his hand to Sarah rather formally. "I'll see you tomorrow morning, Sarah." She winced visibly at the firm handshake. He looked down at her tiny hand enveloped in his huge one and said, "See there—I'm already treating you like one of the guys."

Melanie gave directions to the motel with a smooth confidence that surprised Sarah. Obviously she was smarter than she pretended to be. She would have to be more than merely decorative, Sarah thought grudgingly, to keep the interest of a man like Ian MacDonald. On the heels of that thought she remembered some of Bob Smithfield's comments about Ian's thoughts on women and wondered how much was true.

Sarah made an effort to stop thinking about

her new boss and listen to what Melanie was telling her about apartments, condominiums, and other housing possibilities. She found herself ridiculously pleased to see the dark roots that were nearly hidden by Melanie's carefully bleached hair.

At Sarah's suggestion Melanie called the agent who handled listings at one of the more luxurious beachfront condominiums. Sarah suspected that she'd better not count on work contacts to provide her social life, and she knew that such a living arrangement would insure that she would meet a crowd of other young singles. The less she thought about people at work, the better. She was pleased when Melanie turned from the phone to announce that they did have a one-bedroom unit for rent and set up an appointment to have a look.

The available apartment was perfect. Like the one she had shared with Barbara, it had a balcony with a spectacular view, this time overlooking the Gulf of Mexico. It would be available in about a month. Sarah happily wrote a check for her deposit. Ian MacDonald should be glad to have her settled in quickly, so that there would be no distractions on the job. She would tell him tomorrow and make arrangements to have her furniture shipped.

She would have to spend her first few weekends furniture shopping again—it made her somewhat homesick to realize that Barbara would be doing the same. It had taken them months of careful searching to achieve their apparently casual eclectic blend of antiques and modern, which had now been divided up. Sarah realized with a start that their friends had been the same sort of interesting mix and that replacing friends was going to take a lot longer than replacing furniture. She realized to what extent she was truly starting over.

Sarah had had every intention of using the rest of the afternoon to begin exploring Galveston, but when she checked into her motel room, the large double bed looked so inviting that she lay down with a magazine. The strain of the drive, deciding on the apartment, and, most of all, the interview with MacDonald finally caught up with her, and in a few minutes she was fast asleep.

It was the phone that awakened Sarah. It took her a few moments to realize where she was and a few more to recognize the deep voice at the other end of the line.

"Oh, Mr. MacDonald."

She could have sworn she heard a chuckle. "Ian, please. If you're going to be one of the boys, you'll have to treat me just as the rest of the crew does—and an oil rig is not noted for its formality."

"All right—Ian. Is there some change in plans for the morning?"

"That's better. No, nothing like that. I wanted to see how you made out apartment hunting. And I'm just finishing up at the office. I haven't had dinner yet, and I could use some company. You can tell me about your afternoon over a lobster."

Sarah couldn't decide whether to be annoyed or amused. He had told her just this afternoon that he didn't date members of his crew. Besides, he was making this sound like an order. She couldn't resist saying, "Wouldn't it have been simpler to find out about my apartment search by taking Melanie out to dinner?"

"Well, I'll be darned! Not only am I stuck with a female, but it's a jealous one at that."

That called for a quick response. She certainly couldn't leave him with such a misleading impression. "I'm sorry, Mr. MacDonald . . . Ian. It's just that I was under the impression that you wanted to keep things between us on a strictly business basis."

"Sarah, this *is* strictly business. It's going to be a business dinner. If I even thought of anything else, you'd probably scream sexual harassment. Now—are you interested in a lobster or not?"

Minutes later Sarah stood in the shower, allowing the tiredness of the day to wash away.

She realized that she really was hungry, but she still doubted the wisdom of going out to dinner with Ian MacDonald.

True to his word, Ian discussed business throughout the scrumptious dinner. It was Sarah who had trouble concentrating on drilling for oil. The restaurant overlooked the Gulf, and a spectacular sunset made it an evening designed for romance.

She had felt a bit guilty as she picked one of her slinkier dresses from the small assortment that had traveled with her, and she wondered just why she had chosen to wear her hair loose and flowing. Surely she wasn't falling into the trap of trying to prove to MacDonald that she was feminine; she was going to have enough trouble proving that she was a competent engineer. But his eyes had lit up when he saw her, and she felt a little thrill run down her spine.

Ian ushered her out the door and helped her into, of all things, a pickup truck. As they drove to the restaurant, she glanced around. The pickup did seem to be a widespread feature here, a part of the Texas landscape that she had not really noticed until now. There were obviously plenty of things that would take some adjustment for a transplanted Northerner, and riding in a pickup while dressed for dining in a fancy restaurant was probably the least of them.

She sat across the table from him, trying not to study him too obviously. She had never met a man like this, and she couldn't quite decide how she felt about him—not that it mattered, of course, since it was perfectly obvious how he felt about her. *He* was not the one having trouble concentrating on business.

"What made you decide to become a petroleum engineer?" he finally asked after exhausting the topic of the new deep-water well.

There was a long pause as Sarah tried to decide how much of her background she wanted to discuss with this man. Finally she said, "I was always good in math and science. My teachers and my parents encouraged me to be an engineer. We never had much money, and it seemed like a profession that would pay well."

"Why not medicine? If you were good in math and science and wanted to make a lot of money, I would have thought that being a doctor was a better bet."

"I didn't mean to make it sound as if it were just the money," Sarah protested. "I spent one summer during my high-school years at a 'Women in Engineering' program at a technical institute near home. By the end of the summer I was completely sold."

He nodded as if that made some sense. "I suppose that program put all those other feminist ideas into your head too."

She bristled. "If you mean feminist ideas such as equal opportunity and equal pay, no— I had those long before, thank you."

He reached over and covered her hand with his. "You're pretty when you're angry. Anyone ever tell you that?"

For a business dinner this was clearly getting out of hand. Sarah made an attempt to shift the subject away from herself. "And you?" she asked. "Is this what you really want to do, or did your father just assume that you'd carry on the family business?"

"No, it was my choice. In fact, I've got an older brother who wasn't interested. Andrew's a lawyer. Does a little work for us—he's the one who advised us to hire you, by the way— but he's really not very involved with the company.

"My father emigrated from Scotland when he was only eighteen—you might have guessed something like that from the names that Andy and I were blessed with. The old man started out as a wildcatter—a prospector for oil. He got lucky and hit a gusher, which led to MacDonald Oil. The original field in the northern corner of the state has thirteen wells, all still delivering. They call it black gold, you know, and it has certainly been that for us.

"We're a small company by oil-business standards. A couple of the giants have offered to buy us out several times, but we're not interested. We can make a profit on marginal wells—like the ones offshore here. We'd like to get into some new technologies; one of the reasons we were interested in you was your background in oil shale.

"Dad wanted his sons to have the formal training that he never did, and so he sent me off to college to become a proper petroleum engineer. Then the scoundrel put me in charge of a new division of the business, drilling for offshore oil, while he hightailed it back to Scotland to work on a rig in the North Sea owned by an old friend of his. He's having a ball; I'm sometimes not so sure that I am! I've worked on his rigs since I was in high school, and I've never quite gotten over feeling like a part of the crew rather than the boss. This office work is new for me, and I don't think I'm going to like it."

After having spent well over an hour earlier in the evening listening to him ramble on about the new well, Sarah could tell how much he loved being on the rig. She could listen to him talk about it forever. . . . She caught herself in midthought. It was clear enough that he wanted to keep things between them strictly business.

"C'mon, Sarah," he said, leaving a large bill on the table as he stood up. "We've got a big day tomorrow."

Sarah didn't want an awkward moment at the door of her motel while she fumbled through her purse for her key, so she already had it in her hand as he walked her to the door. "Good night, Ian," she said as she put the key in the lock. "Thank you for a lovely evening."

Once again his hand closed over hers. His other hand lifted her chin, and he looked at her strangely. "This is certainly going to be interesting," he muttered.

For a moment she thought, oddly, that he was going to kiss her. She shut her eyes for an instant in anticipation and then opened them again as he dropped his arms. She was grateful that the darkness hid her blush as he walked away with a casual wave.

Sarah flopped herself on the bed, her emotions in a turmoil. Ian might be prepared to treat her like one of the boys, but he roused emotions in her that she'd never felt before. *Ridiculous!* she thought. Why did it have to be Ian? Why did it have to be her boss, a man with whom she would have to work closely every day? Why did it have to be a man who obviously had never dealt with a professional woman? Sarah vowed to be rational about it. She would just will that attraction to disappear.

When the alarm clock went off and she thought of the restless night she'd spent, she had a feeling that her ability to be logical was about to meet its strongest test.

Chapter Two

*I*F Ian noticed the circles under Sarah's eyes the next morning, he made no comment. He looked approvingly at her coveralls and boots. Her hair was carefully pinned up, ready to tuck under the hard hat that she carried in her hand. He was all business as he ushered her into the truck, and he was filled with comments about the rig as they drove to the dock. She knew that he was seeing her as one of the boys. If she had imagined even a hint of anything else the previous evening, there was certainly no trace of it today.

The launch was already filled with the crew when they arrived. Ian jumped in, called for her to follow, and gave orders to cast off. It was a brisk forty-five-minute ride to the drilling platform, with the wind making any conversation or introductions impossible.

Ian had talked at length about the rig during dinner last night, and still Sarah was not prepared for the reality. If this, as Ian claimed, was a small rig, she could scarcely imagine a large one. Its legs were supported by huge pontoons, and the unfinished derrick itself towered four or five stories above the platform. Ian had told her that it was about two-thirds completed.

She tried to imagine how enormous it would be in another week or so. She knew, in a textbook-knowledge sort of way, that it might have to go even higher, if they had not hit oil by the time they had fed that length of drilling pipe down through the platform and into the seabed. But nothing in her textbooks had prepared her for the thrill that she felt as they approached the huge structure. This was the real thing! She was exhilarated by her first real adventure away from a desk and into the field.

They climbed the ladder of the platform. The two men who made up the midnight security crew boarded a small speedboat, the *Esmerelda,* for the ride back to port. Ian finally called the day crew together and introduced Sarah to them. She saw a few belligerent faces, especially on some of the older men, and caught a few vicious whispered comments, but most of the crew at least made an attempt to greet her warmly.

Sarah knew that she would be fairly useless for the first few days—maybe even for the first few weeks. Her job at the moment was to observe and learn.

She soon discovered that Ian was a master

teacher. He knew every aspect of the project, both from a theoretical and a practical standpoint. He knew all the men well and knew exactly when to praise, when to criticize, and when to keep his mouth shut.

He was no white-collar supervisor. He clambered over the huge rig with his men, helping out whenever he could be useful while he kept an eye on the overall picture. Sarah enjoyed watching him, watching the muscles ripple under his coveralls as he turned valves and climbed ladders. At the end of the day she was as exhausted as if she had been making all of those maneuvers herself.

She stripped off her coveralls and took off her hard hat before stepping into the car. She pulled the pins from her hair and let it come tumbling down, stretching her neck to get out the kinks that had settled there from spending most of the day keeping an eye on the activities near the top of the derrick.

Ian gave a quick glance at her slim body, her jeans and tailored shirt, but he made no comment. His face seemed to display conflicting emotions. Sarah realized that she should have waited until she got home before shedding her outer work clothes. Now she had caused him to shift gears again. He had spent the day concentrating on whether or not she was an adequate engineer. If she wanted to impress him with her professional qualifications, maybe—at least temporarily—she would have to avoid reminding him that after hours she metamorphosed into a female.

Ian was quiet on the ride back to the motel. Sarah couldn't decide if she was disappointed or relieved when he made no move to get out of the car when he pulled up to her door. "You know the way now, Sarah," he said. "You can drive to the launch yourself tomorrow. Remember, it leaves at seven-fifteen sharp."

She opened the car door. He said, "Wait a minute. I just wanted to thank you for keeping out of my hair today."

Sarah was exhausted from her first day on the job. She had been half hoping that he would suggest dinner again and was now feeling disappointed as that seemed unlikely. "Did you expect that I'd follow you around like some puppy?" she snapped.

He grinned. "I know you're tired, Sarah, but don't get huffy. How was I supposed to know what you might do? I've never had a woman on a rig before."

Sarah made an effort to meet him halfway. "I owe you a thank-you too. You gave the crew the impression that you thought I could handle the job."

Ian, who was every bit as tired as she was, exploded. "I never said that you couldn't. But remember, that doesn't mean that I think you belong there. Some of those men think that women on a rig are like women on a ship—just plain bad luck. I've never even had a female visitor on that rig before, and now look what I'm stuck with! If you think I'm happy about it just because I'm putting on a good show for the men . . . *they* have to have complete confidence in you. If I let them know what I was really thinking, I'd undermine the morale of the whole operation!"

Sarah was somewhat shaken by that outburst. She had been lulled into some false sense of accomplishment by Ian's polite professional behavior during the day. She should have known better. He'd made it clear at the beginning that the old-timers like his father—and maybe some of the younger men as well—felt that women on a rig were bad luck. She'd been foolish to think that he would discount their opinions based on one uneventful day with her working at his side.

She tried to lighten the moment. "Remember," she quipped, "you promised to consider me to be just one of the boys."

She turned to leave, but he pulled her toward him and kissed her lightly. She was too surprised to respond.

"That was just to remind me," he said.

Sarah stood with her fingers touched to her lips as she watched him drive away.

By the end of the second day Ian was convinced that Sarah had caught on to all of the techniques and problems associated with the initial stage—the building of the rig. "Would you like to go down in the Submersible tomorrow?" he asked.

Sarah looked at him in surprise. "Surely all of the core samples have been taken," she said, raising an eyebrow.

"The core samples for Rig Number One and Rig Number Two have been taken," he replied, "and some preliminary samples have been taken about midway between. What I'd like to do today, though, is head just a little farther out. If we put our permanent platform out where I'm heading today, we could still easily reach Rigs One and Two by directional drilling, so it's worth exploring. Besides," he said with a grin, "you need to learn as many of the job operations as you can—and things are slow enough this week that I've got the time to show you how it's done."

Sarah was excited about underwater exploration in this diving-bell type of apparatus. It was like entering another world—a world of muted greens and dark shadows, peopled by huge fish making their way silently through the murky waters. Ian was at his best; she was beginning to recognize that he was fun to be with when he was expounding on his favorite subject—drilling for oil.

Ian put Sarah through the paces for the rest of the week. As part of her training he had her doing every possible job until he felt that she had mastered the techniques and seen something of the pitfalls. Sarah enjoyed it immensely. It was good to be doing something physical instead of just pushing papers.

When she was at the top of the rig, she felt on top of the world. On a clear day she could just see the outline of the high beachfront hotels back on Galveston Island and, in the other direction, a hint of the Mexican Yucatan peninsula. Secured by the heavy safety harness, she was happy enough to stay at the top of the rig for hours.

The men were patient with her, and although she noted some grumbling, it didn't seem any worse than those long-ago days when she was a university freshman. And, little by little, she noted the grudging respect from these men just as she had from her professors and classmates as she proved that she was a fast learner and not afraid of hard work.

Actually, Sarah was all too aware that this phase of her training was the easy part. Sooner or later, she knew, she would be expected to take over some of the responsibility, and then she and Ian would be bound to rub each other the wrong way. There was no way that two such strong-minded individuals could share the job of supervising a large crew without having some real differences of opinion. She was trying hard to learn how he handled each problem so that she could issue orders in agreement with his as much as possible. He had actually been very patient with her so far, but she was certain that that couldn't last.

Ian called Sarah aside on Friday. "Come sailing with me tomorrow. We'll discuss the rig and make sure that all your questions are answered. It won't be too long before you're going to have to earn your keep."

Sarah wished that he had phrased it as an invitation rather than a command. He was her boss, though, and it was certainly true that she would appreciate a chance to go over everything she had learned that week. She tried to sound professional and polite. "That's a good idea, Ian. I'll try to spend this evening going over all the procedures and formulating my questions."

He looked at her oddly, and she wondered what his plans for the evening were. Surely they had to be more interesting than going over procedures and formulating questions. She found herself wishing, not for the first time, that he *would* think of her as a woman. *But you can't have it both ways,* she chided herself. *This is a man who likes his women as women, his engineers as engineers—and never the twain shall meet.* She wondered what it would take to change that opinion and then realized that she would probably never get a chance to find out.

The next day Ian arrived promptly at two to pick her up. She caught his glance at her legs, and she was glad that she was wearing a sweatshirt over her skimpy bikini. She had hesitated about the swimsuit. She was beginning to recognize that she didn't really want him to be thinking of her as just one of his engineers, but she knew that wearing the bikini was perhaps a childish way of making her point. In truth, though, it was the only suit that she owned, so she swallowed her qualms. After all, what else would she wear on a sailboat?

The Sunfish skimmed along under Ian's expert guidance. The sun beat down, and Sarah eventually shed her sweatshirt. She tried to pretend that she didn't notice either Ian's scrutiny or his little nod that seemed to indicate she met with his approval. Gradually, as she automatically shifted to help him handle the sails of the small boat, Sarah could feel her tension draining away. The wind and the sun worked their magic, leaving her feeling more relaxed than she had since arriving in Galveston.

She slathered a sun block over her pale Northern skin, laughing in response to his comment that she'd never look like a proper Texan if she used that stuff.

"If I don't, I won't look like a Texan, anyway," she replied, "unless you had in mind a Texan lobster! These transitions from Northerner to Southerner take time," she added more seriously as she compared her pale complexion to his own deep tan.

Gradually she forgot to worry about what he thought of her; she watched admiringly as he skillfully maneuvered the small boat. The sun turned the sandy color of his hair to gold. She tried to remain oblivious to his rugged physique, tried not to be too obvious as she indulged in a little scrutiny of her own.

"In another week I expect to be able to leave you in charge of the day shift on the rig," he yelled to her over the wind.

She sat bolt upright in surprise. She had expected him to stay in charge, with her carrying out duties under his supervision. "Why?" she asked. "Where are you going?"

"Back to the office, where I belong," he said, sounding as if the prospect were not at all a pleasant one.

"You mean that you hired me so you'd be

free to work in the office?" Her mind was spinning rapidly. She had worried about spending her days working with him, knowing that sooner or later they would have a professional clash. Apparently, she wouldn't have that problem.

Would there be another set of problems? With the men? And what would this do to her relationship—if there was to be one—with Ian? If she weren't seeing him every day, perhaps she *could* see him in the evenings. Perhaps he could forget about her daytime role and see her only as an attractive female.

No—not when she spent her days in charge of his "baby"—his multimillion-dollar rig. He would never be able to forget his worries about her engineering abilities.

Sarah shook her head and tuned herself back to Ian in time to catch the answer to her question.

"Somebody has to carry out the duties of president of this organization. Like it or not, I seem to have been elected."

"But, Ian, you enjoy working on the rig so much! Couldn't you have hired a business manager to take care of the office work?"

"Believe it or not, I tried. We've been on a search for someone to serve as acting president. It will take a special person, and we never expected to fill the position in a hurry. Just in case it took a long time, we were also looking for an engineer who could be trained for the supervisory position. That would free me—if that's what you would call it—to work in the office. You were interviewed as part of that search. But it was always understood that we couldn't fill both positions this year. Until the well comes in, there just isn't enough money.

"Shortly after your interview we actually felt that we had found the right person for the job as acting president. We hired him, but it didn't work out, and I found myself trying to handle both jobs again. We were actively searching for another business manager when our lawyers advised us that we'd better hire you if we didn't want a lengthy and expensive suit on our hands. So I'm back in the office, and you're in charge of the rig."

"You mean that because you hired me, you can't hire a business manager—and you're stuck with a job you dislike?" No wonder their relationship had started off on such a sour note!

"At the moment, yes. But don't look so distressed, Sarah. I told you that we'd been interviewing for both positions. When we bring in Number One, we'll be in better shape financially. Then when Number Two well is ready for start-up this winter, I'll try again to find someone to take over the office work so I can be on that rig."

He fell silent again as the wind kicked up and the sailboat demanded more of his attention. Sarah thought about what he had said. In another week he would be back in the onshore office—with Melanie—and she would be in charge of the crew. She knew exactly what they were doing—he had made sure of that. And she had supervised a small staff in her last job, so she was not worried about her abilities in that direction—not *too* worried, anyway, though she had to admit that these men seemed, like their boss, more antifemale than her colleagues in the East.

She wondered how some of the older men would react when the reality of a female boss became apparent. She had no doubt that she was capable enough, but she was surprised that Ian thought that she was. Well, she had asked for it. At least she wouldn't have the distraction of working so closely with Ian.

The breeze began to fade as evening approached, and Ian began to tack back toward the southwest end of the island. "Stupid of me," he said as he beached the boat near his house. "I forgot to tell you to bring some clothes. We'll have to go back to your motel so you can change for dinner. I'll fix you a drink, and you can relax while I get dressed. There's no point in driving back this way—the restaurant I had in mind is down at your end of the island."

Typical, Sarah thought. His invitation to dinner was issued as another order. Still, they hadn't yet discussed the rig and Sarah's questions, so it was really not unreasonable to assume that she was still "on duty."

Sarah was stunned by Ian's house; it was one of the biggest on the island. She had assumed that the president of MacDonald Oil wouldn't be living in poverty, but this was ridiculous. This house must have six or seven bedrooms— and Ian lived here by himself!

Sarah had barely finished her drink when Ian reappeared, hair still wet from the shower but otherwise impeccably dressed. She felt foolish in her swimsuit and sweatshirt, her hair salty from the windy spray.

She felt even more foolish as they approached her motel later. She wasn't exactly set up for entertaining guests; she couldn't even offer him a drink while she showered.

He might have been reading her thoughts. "It's not quite like home, is it, Sarah?" he volunteered. "I'll give you some privacy while you get ready. I could use a drink myself, anyway. Half hour be okay?" She nodded gratefully as he headed to the motel lounge.

A while later Sarah was just brushing her hair when Ian knocked lightly and stepped into the room. He came over to her and put his hands on her shoulders, left bare by her halter-style silk dress, and kissed her lightly. "You're beautiful," he said. Sarah felt the warm glow beginning again.

They danced after dinner, on a balcony over-looking the water. The moon cast silver shadows on the gentle waves. Ian was nearly a foot taller than Sarah, but she fit into his arms as if she were meant to be there. Snuggling up to his broad chest made her feel protected and cherished. She could feel his breath in her hair whenever he talked to her, and it sent little shivers running down her spine.

They drove back to her motel in silence. It had been a special evening. Something was happening to their relationship. They had managed not to antagonize each other for nearly a whole day. Neither, she realized belatedly, had they discussed the business that had presumably been the object of their day together. That was it, of course. He had been thinking of her as a woman today and not as an engineer. That should have made Sarah happy, but it didn't. What she wanted was for him to realize that she could be both at once—not for him to become schizophrenic about it.

He walked her to her door and stood there as if uncertain. Sarah was as uncertain as he and unwilling to break the spell. She took a deep breath and reluctantly said what she knew she had to say. "You're coming in, aren't you?" she asked in a businesslike tone. "Delightful though it's been, we've been goofing off all day. We were supposed to be going over the procedures and working on my list of questions—I've got even more now that I know that after next week I'll be in charge! We can call room service for a pot of coffee and plunge in."

He took her chin in his hand and lifted it, gazing into her eyes for a long moment. "Not tonight, Sarah. I can't make the transition tonight. I'd rather not think of you as my second-in-command right now. For tonight just let me think of you as a woman."

So she'd been right in thinking that he had problems in dealing with the possibility of a combination. Somehow the smug feeling that she could reasonably expect as a reward for her perception didn't materialize. All she could think of was that he *was,* for however briefly, seeing her as a woman. She was ready to melt into his arms, but he kissed her lightly and waved good-bye.

Ian called her in the morning. "I suppose I should apologize for taking up your entire weekend," he began, "but I think we really should get together today and cover the matters that we never got to yesterday."

This morning he was the one who sounded quite businesslike, and Sarah felt a stab of disappointment. She would have to make up her mind, she realized, whether she wanted him as a supervisor or as a romantic interest. It was not going to be possible to have both. If she made the decision, then maybe she could set the tone to produce the desired effect. If she left it up to him, they would continue this schizophrenic merry-go-round. At the moment, though, she had no option but to match his mood.

"I should be the one to apologize, for taking up *your* whole weekend," she said. "It's nice of you to spend the time making sure that I know what I'm doing."

He snorted. He was certainly his best oilman self this morning. "Nice of me? I'm just protecting my investment—and I don't mean in you. That's a multimillion-dollar rig I'm putting you in charge of! Dumbest thing I've ever done, but I really don't have any choice. The office can't run itself forever."

Sarah heard the chill creep into her own voice as she replied. "If you think it's so dumb, why do it? Why not just fire me and hire someone you think can handle the job?"

"Come off it, Sarah. You know what I think

of your competence, and so do all the men on the rig. You'd have the makings of one devil of a lawsuit if I fired you now. You know my feelings; you don't belong on that rig. But my chances of getting you off it are zero, so I've got to use you as if you were a man. Now let's try to get back to thinking of you as one of the boys—the one who will be in charge of the whole shebang in a little over a week. I'll pick you up in an hour; we'll work at my place today."

Sarah had a little trouble deciding what to wear. The weather certainly demanded brevity, and she started out with a flattering lavender outfit—shorts and a matching halter top. Then, as if realizing what she was doing, she exchanged the top for a more modest T-shirt and replaced her strappy sandals with more practical sneakers. There was no doubt that Ian meant to keep his mind on business today. What did the proper young engineer wear on a Sunday afternoon when discussing business with the boss? She breathed a sigh of relief when she glanced out the motel window and saw Ian leap out of the pickup, clad in white jogging shorts and striped terry shirt.

Ian's house was at the southwest end of the island, away from the congestion of Galveston proper. As they drove out of town on the road paralleling the Gulf, the houses became larger and more impressive. There was some striking contemporary architecture, with interesting angles and decks providing spectacular views of the water.

As he turned into his own drive, her impression of the day before, when they had approached his house from the rear as they beached the boat, was confirmed. His house was one of the largest and most impressive, even in this affluent area.

"Isn't this house a little big for you?" she asked. "You must feel as if you're rattling around in a mansion."

He grinned. "I do. But the land was for sale at a good price—we'll never see that type of bargain again, with the surge in real estate values that this area is experiencing. I needed a place to live, so it made sense to have the house built. It was a bit premature, I admit. But I expect to fill it up eventually." He caught her puzzled look and laughed. "Children, Sarah. You look as if the thought had never occurred to you. Ah, you professional women!"

"Children." She repeated it, stupidly.

"Yes. Children. You know, little people. The stork brings them. I'd like about six."

Sarah made an effort not to gulp audibly. "Six. . . ." she said in what she hoped was a fairly normal voice. "How nice. Melanie is in agreement with this, I suppose?"

He laughed. "There you go again, making assumptions about my relationship with Melanie. You're better trained than that; why don't you show it and stop basing your conclusions on insufficient data?"

Sarah blushed at her own lapse into betraying her jealousy, as well as at the deserved snipe at her nonscientific assumptions. She hurried to change the subject. Fumbling in her briefcase, she brought out a notepad and a neatly typed list. "Shall we get started?" she asked. "Now, the first thing that I don't feel really certain about is. . . ."

She saw the businesslike mask drop down again over Ian's eyes. It was almost as if . . . almost as if he had not been overly anxious to plunge into work. This time it was she who had made the shift back to business, and he had taken the cue. She could have bitten off her tongue, but it was too late to backtrack. She concentrated hard on the questions she had for Ian, carefully took notes as he answered, and had completely run out of material in a little over an hour.

"Well," he said coolly, "it seems that I don't need to take up your whole day after all." He stood up and took his car keys from his pocket.

It was obvious that their work session was at an end.

Sarah made a last-ditch effort to detain him, scolding herself as she did so. Why couldn't she let it go? Maybe he did vacillate in his perception of her, but she knew that at least half the fault was hers. He had treated her like a professional colleague today; there had been no snide remarks about female engineers. Why not settle for that? Why did she keep trying for more? She pushed the nagging questions out of her mind as she purposefully stopped to admire a painting in the living room, making no move to follow him as he headed for the door.

"Like it?" he asked casually.

"Yes. Who's the artist?"

"Local fellow. I have several of his. That one over the piano, one in the dining room, a couple in the den . . . would you like to see those?"

There was just a trace of hesitation in his offer, and Sarah felt a perverse surge of satisfaction. She wanted him to stay confused about her for at least as long as she was confused about him. "Yes," she said in a level voice. "I'd like to see them."

The den, like the rest of the house, was furnished tastefully and expensively. One of the paintings hung over a low leather sofa, another over a teak desk. Like the one in the living room, these showed waterbirds along the marshy shore. Sarah had initially pretended more interest than she felt, but now she was finding that she really was impressed.

Ian broke the silence. "These are scenes that I see every morning from the deck. Perhaps it seems silly to have the paintings as well, but I do think he's captured the whole thing beautifully. I suspect that his work will be worth something someday, but I wasn't thinking of the investment when I bought these. Though," he added with a grin, "it's always good public relations to support the local craftsmen."

He ushered her out the door, any thoughts of lingering obviously nonexistent—at least for him. He took her arm to help her into the truck. Until she had arrived in Galveston, Sarah realized, she hadn't been helped into a car in years. She found that she had been enjoying this Southern graciousness and favored him with a smile of appreciation.

Ian seemed to shift mental gears again. "If you have no plans for the rest of the day, I'd enjoy showing you around the island."

Sarah was taken completely by surprise. "Why . . . why, no. I'd thought that our work session would take much longer, so I left the whole day free. But just because we were so marvelously efficient doesn't mean that you have to tie up the rest of your day. . . ."

He turned and grinned at her. "I left the rest

of the day free too. We may as well keep each other company."

It was hardly a romantic remark, but it was more than she had expected. She allowed herself a small smile of satisfaction.

They started out with a tram ride that provided a guided tour. Ian added his own commentary on some of the restored Victorian houses. "That one's worth seeing." Or, much to Sarah's delight, "We'll have to visit that one someday."

At the northeastern end of the island Sarah expressed amazement at Ian's skill in driving directly onto the beach without getting the car mired in the sand. They walked along the jetty hand in hand. Sarah tried to adjust to this mood of Ian's as she had tried at other times to adjust to him when he was dealing with her as an unwanted female engineer. He seemed interested enough in her when he could forget that she worked for him in what he considered to be a man's job.

They strolled in silence. Sarah tried hard to be rational. There was no sense in getting involved with a man who felt that women belonged at home . . . with six children, no less. If only she hadn't seen his good side! It was impossible not to like him when she watched him at work, admiring his skill and patience. It was impossible to claim that he was insensitive when his house was filled with paintings of marsh birds and when his love of the land was as evident as it was now as he enthusiastically pointed out jellyfish and crabs hiding along the jetty.

It was impossible not to catch his boyish love of life as he sailed the Sunfish. It was even impossible to resist the smooth Southern charm, try though she might to remind herself that it went hand in hand with an attitude toward women that in the North would be called chauvinism.

It was impossible to miss his sense of humor; he laughed even at himself and at the predicament in which he found himself with his female engineer. Added to all that was his devastating good looks and the sheer physical attraction she felt every time he smiled at her.

And then there was the fact that he was her boss. Even if there were no other problems—even if he had automatically accepted her as engineer *and* woman, all rolled up in one package rather than one during the day and another after working hours—Sarah knew that it was the height of foolishness to become involved with the company president. She was going to have enough trouble winning over the men without having them think that she had an inside edge with Ian. They might even think that he'd hired her because of their relationship. If only they knew just how funny that was!

Sarah knew that romantic liaisons were best carried on far away from the workplace in any event—whether the man in question was her supervisor or not. She had succeeded in her profession by being coolly efficient on the job— hardly a demeanor calculated to attract the men with whom she worked. Her dates had usually been men she and Barbara had met in other ways—others who lived in the condominium, old friends from college, a couple of young lawyers from Barbara's firm. . . .

Sarah brought her thoughts back to reality. There was no point in worrying about a relationship with Ian when it didn't seem likely that one was developing. He had made it clear that he didn't approve of female engineers. He seemed able to block out her profession from his mind when he saw her outside of work, but that was hardly a satisfactory arrangement. At the moment she was a curiosity, but eventually he would tire of trying to decide where the engineer left off and the woman began.

She should call a halt to the whole thing right now. If she didn't want to get involved with him, there was an easy-enough solution. She could just let him think that she had no feminine attributes at all. She could stop rising to the bait, stop trying to let him see the side of her that she was showing now. She could concentrate on proving herself on the job.

She glanced up at him and felt her stomach lurch in a way that was becoming all too familiar. It was easy enough to say that she wanted merely to be a respected colleague, but Sarah knew that what she really wanted was to feel those strong arms around her once again. Sarah had a problem, and she knew it.

Sarah and Ian ate dinner at a casual home-style cafeteria near the seawall, for which their outfits of shorts and sneakers were appropriate; then they finished off the day as foot passengers on the free ferry that plied its way back and forth between the port of Galveston and the less crowded Port Bolivar. They stood at the ferry's rail, watching the sun set, watching the sea gulls dip and soar as they scavenged for bread tossed by other passengers. The strident cries of the gulls seemed appropriate background music for the turmoil that Sarah felt.

Ian took her gently into his arms and kissed her, and she felt the tension dissolve. He held her close and whispered, "Oh, Sarah, why can't you be just a woman I met at a party?" Sarah felt calm, somehow reassured by the knowledge that he was as confused as she.

Chapter Three

S ARAH sat in comfortable solitude on the balcony of her motel room, watching the storm clouds roll in. The Gulf was as rough as the Atlantic; her usual after-work swim had been real exercise tonight as she rode each foamy breaker in to shore.

The telephone interrupted her solitude. Ian, of course. There was still really no one else who might be calling. Her throat constricted as she heard the familiar deep, husky voice.

"I'm coming over," he said. "We'll need to discuss plans for tomorrow."

"Tomorrow?" She had thought she knew exactly what would be going on. The derrick was proceeding on schedule. In another two weeks—this one still under Ian's supervision, the next one on her own—they should be ready for drilling.

"The storm," he said patiently, as if talking to a very young child. "The storm changes everything. Blast it all! It's too early in the season for a tropical storm like this."

"Is it expected to be a bad storm?" she asked innocently.

"Sarah." His exasperation was evident as he nearly spat the word. "Don't you listen to the news? To the weather reports? Haven't you looked out the window? Have you seen the Gulf?"

"I was sitting on the balcony when you called. I was swimming in the Gulf not an hour ago. I love it when it's rough like this. It was just like swimming in the Atlantic . . . but of course it's so wonderfully warm."

"Stop sounding like a Northern tourist, for Pete's sake! You're living *here* now, on a barrier island. We're in a hurricane watch, and you're out casually bobbing over the waves! Everybody else in Galveston is glued to a radio or TV, and you're sitting out on the balcony watching the storm roll in!"

She resisted the impulse to continue raving on about how beautiful it was. "A hurricane watch? There's a hurricane heading this way?"

"Let's hope not," he said sternly. "The watch is just the first stage. It's too early yet to tell whether or not the storm will blow itself out before it hits land or where the landfall will be if it doesn't. We'll know later tonight. If it seems to be heading for us, they'll change the status to 'hurricane warning.' If it gets that far, it'll be time to batten down the hatches. You've noticed the storm shutters on the door to your balcony? They're there for a reason.

"If it looks like a direct hit," he continued as she listened in unbelieving fascination, "they'll evacuate the island—and you and I will be lucky to have a home to come back to. Your motel, the apartment you've just rented, *and* my house were built since the last hurricane, so there's no telling whether they've a chance of survival. Many have said that Galveston has been too heavily built up—that a barrier island like this should have been left mainly undisturbed. The whole city was wiped out once, back around the turn of the century. It was after that that the seawall was built, in the hopes of preventing another disaster.

"You've noticed that the older houses on the island are all raised? The garages are on the first level, with living quarters starting at the second story. The memory of the great storm was still fresh in people's minds when those houses were built. We've become more complacent lately. At my end of the island there isn't even a seawall."

Sarah's fascination was slowly turning to horror as she pictured the raging waters washing over the southwest end of the island, sweeping away everything in their path as they covered the small strip of land between gulf and bay.

"And the rig?" She barely whispered the question, afraid to hear his answer.

"That's what I want to talk about. I'll be over in ten minutes. I'm at the office now."

"Have you had dinner?" It didn't sound as if he'd given any thought to mundane things like that.

He paused. She could picture him standing there, trying to remember when he'd last eaten. "No," he said finally.

"Neither have I," she said. "I'll call out for a pizza. We can eat while we talk."

She heard him sigh. Perhaps he was so worried—about his house and the rig—that mentioning food had been inappropriate. "You're good for me, Sarah," he said, almost reluctantly. "Eating is a good idea. A pizza is a good idea. I'll stop for some beer."

He hung up the phone abruptly. She stood there holding her telephone, amazed once again at his shift in mood.

Ian and the pizza arrived almost simultaneously. He looked around the small motel room. "Let's eat out on the balcony," he suggested. "We can watch your exciting waves while we discuss what to do when they're five times as high."

Ian turned up the volume of the TV set so it could be heard from the balcony. Sarah was mesmerized by the weather reports, and Ian seemed hypnotized by the crashing waves. He opened a bottle of beer and handed it to her without comment. They attacked the pizza eagerly, almost as if happy to postpone a discussion of what might lie ahead.

"The rig?" she asked finally, knowing that it had to be uppermost on his mind.

"It may or may not survive a direct hit. This design is supposed to withstand anything, but a similar one was lost off Newfoundland just a couple of years ago. Imagine—a ten-story structure, gone without a trace. Three men were killed."

Sarah gasped. She had been thinking in terms of dollars lost, not in terms of human life.

"That won't happen here," he said. "We know, after that accident, that nothing is guaranteed to survive the elements when they're at their worst. I pulled the two security men off at about six o'clock, as soon as I'd heard the weather reports."

Suppose, like herself, he hadn't been listening to the weather reports? Sarah's blood ran cold at the thought. It was another incident that pointed out her inexperience. Of course Ian would listen to the reports. He was in charge of the rig, in charge of the safety of his men. No, she countered . . . *she* was in charge of the rig and the men—or would be, in another week. She was lucky that pulling in the night guards had not been left up to her.

Ian continued. "If we're lucky, all we'll do is lose a few days' work. If there's no damage, the crew can get right back to building the derrick as soon as the storm has passed. Otherwise. . . ." He shrugged. "Otherwise we start repairing the damage and continue." He stopped talking again to listen to the TV. "From what they're saying, we'll be lucky not to lose the whole thing—the whole million-dollar baby!"

The pizza suddenly tasted stale in her mouth. She put it down and reached for another bottle of beer. He reached over and patted her hand. "Look at those whitecaps now! It *is* pretty, isn't it . . . if you don't think about the destruction it can cause."

She turned stricken eyes to meet his. "Oh, Ian, I'm sorry. I didn't realize . . . I thought it was just going to rain."

He laughed at her embarrassment. "I wasn't being sarcastic, Sarah. It *is* impressive. I built my house on the beach so I could watch the Gulf in all its moods. And this would be one of my favorite ones if I didn't have so much at stake." He stood up and pulled her to her feet. "We've got a couple of hours before we'll hear any real news. C'mon—let's walk along the beach."

*   *   *

It was obvious that Ian shared in Sarah's exhilaration, despite his worries. The strident cries of the gulls could be heard even over the thunder of the crashing surf. The air seemed charged with electricity. They could hear thunder in the distance. An occasional flash of lightning cast an eerie glow over the pale sand.

In silent agreement they walked to the jetty. They were alone on the beach and felt as if they were alone in the world. Everyone else in Galveston was surely still glued to the radio or TV, anxiously waiting for some definitive word on the path of the storm.

The waves were crashing over the rocks of the jetty, making it slippery in places. It was foolishness to be out here, where they could be swept off in an instant if a particularly large wave came along. Whose idea had it been? They seemed to stroll this way together, with neither really taking the lead. Had he let her come out here so she would have a better appreciation of the dangers of the storm?

She glanced up at him and recognized that his love of this raging sea matched her own. They were here because they wanted to be . . . because, despite the danger, there was a feeling of wonder here on the jetty. They were caught up in awe rather than fear. This was nature at its most dramatic, and for a little while they could forget the havoc that it would wreak and enjoy being in the midst of the turmoil.

The wind whipped Sarah's hair across her face. Her eyes stung from the salt spray. She shivered slightly, and he pulled her to him.

His kisses tasted of salt. Little droplets of spray clung to his eyelashes, and she stood on her tiptoes and pulled his face down toward her so that she could kiss them away. He gathered her hair with one hand and twisted it gently, holding it behind her neck so that it would no longer lash out. With his free hand he traced the curve of her cheekbone slowly. The gentleness of his hands seemed somehow incongruous in the midst of the battle of the elements surrounding them.

He pulled her close to him to meet his kiss. She clung to him as if she were drowning, her emotions in greater turmoil than if she had been swept off the jetty and into the churning water.

Sarah wanted to stay there forever. She felt at one with the sea, at one with Ian. They were sharing a closeness she'd never known before. She was brought abruptly to her senses by a huge wave that crashed over the jetty, spraying them with sea foam. Thunder clapped; the lightning streaked. Another wave hit. The spray enveloped them like some salty rain.

She pulled herself away and looked at Ian.

His hair hung down on his forehead, dripping water into his eyes and onto his nose. She knew that she must look the same. He laughed and took her by the hand. "Time to start home, Sarah. This was something special—I've never really had anyone to share it with before."

She felt it too—a magic that she'd never known. But she knew it was about to be shattered, and she braced herself for his next comment.

"Now we get to see the ugly side of all this. Let's see what the prediction is now."

Back inside her motel room, Sarah tossed Ian a bath towel as she retreated to the bathroom to see what she could do with her own hair. She heard the sound of the TV again and came out of the bathroom, comb in hand, to join him in apprehensive waiting.

He stood there toweling his hair, hanging on to every word of the newscast. It was hardly good news. The storm was now a full-blown hurricane named, as seemed about right for this early in the season, Annabelle. Current tracking reports had it heading directly for Galveston, traveling at a speed of fifteen miles per hour. That meant that predicted landfall was at ten in the morning.

Sarah was stunned. The storm was still more than twelve hours away, and already it seemed worse than anything she'd ever encountered. She looked at Ian, her eyes filled with questions.

"I'll have to leave now," he said, as if in response to her unspoken words. "I've got to see to making my own house secure. Then I'll go to the office. There are some storm shutters there that need to be locked into place. It's safer than the house, in any event, since it's a few blocks from the water. And it's closer to the causeway, in case we get the word to evacuate the island. You'll be all right here—just keep the TV on so you can get off the island if the announcement comes.

"If we're still in Galveston tomorrow morning—which would be only if the storm changes direction—come to the office." He grinned. "You might as well continue to earn your keep. Bad enough that the men will get a couple of days off with pay—but you I can use. *If* we can keep our minds on it, we can attack some of the paperwork that still awaits my loving attention."

She tried to match his businesslike tone. They'd had their moment, on the jetty, but now there were things that must be done. She didn't even mind right now if she sounded like an efficient engineer. "Let me come to the house and help you, Ian. There are a lot of shutters to secure. There's nothing I need to do here. We'll just lock the one shutter over the door to the balcony and leave."

He looked at her gratefully. "Good idea. I really could use some help. For a storm that's still so far offshore, this one is packing a wallop. If I don't get the shutters fastened down soon, I'll be missing a lot of glass. Of course," he added ruefully, "I could be missing the whole house by morning. Then we'd have done all this work for nothing."

He headed to the balcony to fasten the shutter, then took Sarah's arm and led her to his pickup truck.

The ride out to the southwestern end of the island seemed interminable. There were trees strewn across the road, and Ian had to skirt them by driving along the sand at the road's edge. Sarah began to see just how useful a four-wheel-drive vehicle could be; her little sports car would have been mired in the soft sand within a few miles of the motel.

By the time they reached Ian's house, the huge expanses of glass on the seaward side were rattling in the fierce wind. She wondered how he would have managed without her; it took all of their combined strength to wrestle with the large custom-fitted shutters. She felt guilty as she realized that he should have been here sooner, instead of standing with her on the jetty.

It took nearly an hour to secure the house. They were both soaked to the skin from the salt spray and the bursts of rain that had begun. It felt warm and cozy when they finally stepped back into the house.

"I've got to shower and get into some dry clothes," he said. "Then we'll get you back to your motel so you can do the same. Make some coffee, will you?"

She got up to head to the kitchen, and he stopped and stared. "No . . . not tonight, Sarah. It was all right for you to sit and wait while I showered after our day on the boat, but tonight you look like a drowned rat . . . a chilly and exhausted rat, at that. You use the upstairs shower while I use the one by my bedroom. *Then* we'll make the coffee."

"But—"

"But what will you wear? I don't know. How about one of my flannel shirts and some sweatpants? They may not be a perfect fit, but they'll be warm and dry. They'll certainly do until we can get you back to your room." He headed to his bedroom as he talked, then returned with an oversized plaid shirt and a pair of sweatpants, which he tossed at her. "Now . . . off to the shower with you."

Sarah headed for the bathroom. The warm

water pounding over her body felt soothing and relaxing. He was right that she was exhausted, but the coffee would help. Perhaps she could help him secure the storm shutters on the office as well. They'd need another shower after that. She should remind him to bring some extra clothes.

She rubbed her skin to a rosy pink and put on the warm shirt and the pants, which were both ludicrously big. She rolled up the bottom of the pants and walked bravely out to the kitchen.

Ian had just filled the coffeepot with water and measured out the coffee. He plugged it in and turned on the small TV that sat on a kitchen shelf. The reporter had spoken about three meaningless words when the lights went off and the TV fell silent.

Ian looked resigned. "I suppose it was expected. Come on. We can listen to the latest on the car radio as we drive back. Sorry about the coffee."

The drive back to the center of Galveston took even longer than the drive out to the end of the island. The weather report wasn't encouraging. The hurricane continued on its relentless course, still headed straight for Galveston. So far there had been no orders to evacuate the island, but the steady stream of traffic headed toward the center of town and the causeway told them that many families, especially from this vulnerable southwest end, were not waiting for official orders.

"I'm taking you to the office with me," Ian said.

Sarah's heart skipped a beat. She had planned to offer to help him again, but it was nice to have him do the offering. "Can we stop at my motel for a change of clothes first?" she asked.

He laughed. "I'd already forgotten that you borrowed my stuff. Shows that my mind is really on this storm, doesn't it? I'm usually very aware of what the lady I'm escorting is wearing."

They were traveling along the main road of the island, along which the seawall had been built so many years before. Sarah's beachfront motel was on this road, just a few miles ahead. About five miles beyond was the new condominium in which she had just rented an apartment.

The palm trees were bending low in the strong wind. There was quite a bit of traffic until they reached the turnoff toward the causeway, and then they suddenly found themselves alone. The houses that they passed didn't seem deserted, but they were shuttered against the storm.

They drove another mile or so in silence,

anxious to get behind strong shutters themselves. Suddenly Ian's headlights focused on some sort of barrier ahead of them in the gloom.

"It's a roadblock!" he said, upset.

Sure enough, a sawhorse stood in the middle of the road. A policeman with a flashlight approached them, rain running in sheets off his rubber mackintosh.

"We're evacuating this end of the island," he said. "It's already over the seawall just ahead."

"We'd just like to pick up some clothes for the lady—" Ian began.

The officer cut him short. "Road's already closed to eastbound traffic, sir. We'll need both lanes for the traffic leaving here. Sorry."

Ian turned to Sarah with a grin. "Sorry about that, Sarah. No clothes until tomorrow—assuming that your motel hasn't washed away by then."

Sarah realized that she had forgotten to remind Ian to bring some extra clothes for himself. The power failure had driven the thought straight from her mind. It appeared that they would both have to make do with what they were wearing. At least he was a little better dressed than she.

The storm seemed less violent as they turned away from the Gulf and headed into town to

Ian's office, though the palms still bent nearly to the ground with each gust of wind. "At least we can get these shutters in place from the inside," Ian commented, and Sarah breathed a sigh of relief.

The office seemed the cheeriest place they'd been in for hours. There were only a few windows, and, as Ian had promised, it was possible to fasten the shutters without tromping around in the storm. Of course they had to open each window, lean out, grab the shutter, and pull it to—all against the raging wind. They were pretty well soaked by the time they finished, but at least this time it was not from a salty spray.

The office was warm and dry, and the electricity was still on in this part of town. Ian turned on a radio near Melanie's desk to get the latest report, and then, obviously pleased with himself over whatever he was about to reveal, walked over to the door of what Sarah had taken to be a closet.

"Coffee," he said proudly as he swung open the door to a tiny kitchenette. "Maybe cookies too. Let's see what Melanie has stashed away in here."

Sarah felt her energy returning as she smelled the coffee brewing. She looked around. She hadn't really paid much attention to the office on the only other occasion that she'd seen it. There was a big leather couch in this room, the outer office, which was Melanie's turf. Was there another in Ian's private office? She couldn't remember. It hardly mattered, anyway. Somehow she couldn't imagine that either of them would sleep that night.

She wrapped her hands around the steaming mug. Her clothes were nearly dry, but she still felt a bit chilled. She had left her sodden sneakers at Ian's house, so her feet were bare.

She turned her attention to the television. Ian sat down beside her on the couch. He at least had shoes on, she noticed. He looked her up and down for the first time, then got up and headed into his office. *That bad?* she wondered.

He came back out carrying a tweed sports jacket, which he handed to her as he sat down again. "Is this supposed to make my outfit complete?" she asked.

"Put it on," he directed. "You've been soaked again. I don't want you to catch pneumonia."

She put the jacket on over the flannel shirt and tucked her feet under her. Ian draped one arm over her shoulder. That, she thought, would produce more of a warming effect than the sports jacket. They settled down, snug and secure for the first time that night, to listen to the reports on the storm.

Sarah found herself nodding off. *Ridiculous,*

she thought, *I'm sitting here in the path of a hurricane and I can't stay awake.* She felt her head drop to Ian's shoulder, felt his arm tighten around her. She was warm and happy, and so tired. . . .

She woke with a start when she felt his arm on her shoulder shift a little. It took her a minute to realize where she was. She saw that Ian was asleep. His long lashes brushed his cheeks, making him look young and vulnerable. She tried to shift a little without waking him and focused again on the radio report. Suddenly she sat up straight. "Ian," she cried, "the storm has turned."

He was instantly as awake as she. The announcer continued, and they sat and listened with increasing relief. There had been an easterly shift, and Annabelle was headed across the Gulf of Mexico. It was expected that most of her force would be spent before she hit Florida's west coast.

They looked at each other as if they couldn't believe their good fortune. As she stared at him, she saw his expression change, grow serious. He reached out again, as he had on the jetty, to run his hand along the line of her cheekbone and on down to her jaw. He lifted her chin and looked longingly at her, and suddenly she was in his arms.

All of Sarah's senses were instantly wide

awake and alive. The whole evening seemed to have been leading up to this. Her fingers twined in his hair where it curled at the nape of his neck. She was lost in the wonder of it all.

The door burst open. "Ian, I thought you'd be here." Melanie's words came in a rush, during the instant before her eyes took in the scene. "Why don't you sleep at my place? It would be much cozier."

They heard her swift intake of breath as she realized that Sarah was there, wrapped in Ian's arms. "Well," she said, "excu-use me. I see that it's pretty cozy here already."

Sarah blushed as she sat up straight and moved away from Ian. Surely Melanie would turn on her heels and stomp off. This must have been as embarrassing to her as it was to them.

Melanie stared at them, her eyes narrowing into slits. She showed no sign of embarrassment and didn't seem anxious to leave. "That's a stunning outfit you're wearing, my dear," she sniped at Sarah.

"Sarah left her clothes at my house," Ian volunteered. Sarah thought that he might have chosen his words with more care. "As a matter of fact, Melanie," he continued, "sleeping at your house is a good idea. But not for me. I'm fine right here, but there really isn't room for two." Melanie raised an eyebrow at that, but he ignored her and went on. "You must have some clothes that will fit Sarah. I'm sure that her motel will still be off limits tomorrow. She can hardly help here in the office, wearing nothing but my clothes. Take her home with you tonight and bring her back in with you in the morning—reasonably clothed."

The two women stared at him in amazement. He couldn't be serious. Sarah would as soon walk into a lion's den. Melanie looked as if she'd like to strangle both of them.

As if he were reading their minds, Ian spoke up again—more forcefully this time. "I meant it. Get moving. We'll have a lot of work to do in the next few days. Just because the storm has changed course doesn't mean there will be no damage. I want everybody fresh and alert first thing in the morning—so get on home and get to bed."

The boss had spoken. Sarah followed Melanie out of the room and into her car.

"I'm sorry that he foisted me off on you," Sarah managed as Melanie slammed into gear and raced out of the parking lot.

"Shut up!" was the reply.

Sarah did just that. After all, there really was nothing more to say.

Melanie's mood hadn't improved by the time they reached her apartment. She tossed a pillow and a blanket at Sarah and said,

"Here. You can sleep on the couch." Exhaustion was catching up to Sarah, and even Melanie's couch looked good. She suspected that Melanie would actually have preferred an out-and-out hair-pulling battle, but Sarah had no energy left even for a rational discussion. She thanked her reluctant hostess, curled up on the sofa, and was asleep even before Melanie left the room.

Sarah was awakened by Melanie's call. "Bathroom's all yours." Somehow the voice didn't sound quite so spiteful this morning.

Sarah stared at herself in the bathroom mirror. It was hopeless. She rummaged in her purse, thankful that she had at least had it along as they headed off to Ian's house. It seemed days ago. She found a comb and a lipstick. She grimaced as she worked the tangles loose from her hair. The wind and rain had really done a job. She stared at her image again. It was hard to believe that last night he had found her desirable. But perhaps he really hadn't. They had shared an experience, that was all—an experience that left them clinging to each other in relief when it was over. It had no doubt meant nothing to him.

Melanie was trying to be nice this morning. "Take a look in the closet and see what you can find, Sarah," she volunteered. "I think almost anything will fit." She looked Sarah up and down, barely repressing a grin as she once again took in Ian's clothes. "At least it will fit better than what you've been wearing. I'm a little taller and a little heavier than you, but it seems to me that you like your clothes a little longer and looser anyway—not as loose as that charming outfit, of course." That time she did stifle a laugh.

"What size shoes do you wear?"

"Five and a half."

"Oh. Well, can't have everything. Still, you can't spend the day padding around the office in your bare feet. Look—how about some backless sandals? It won't matter if there's an extra inch of shoe sticking out the back."

Sarah looked through the closet while Melanie rummaged through the shelves for sandals.

"We should eat breakfast," Melanie said as Sarah finished dressing. "I don't usually, but this could turn out to be a long day. Toast and coffee okay?"

"Sure," Sarah replied. It seemed a long time since she'd eaten. Was it only last night that she and Ian had shared a pizza as they watched the approaching storm?

"Hey, that looks pretty good," Melanie said grudgingly as Sarah came into the kitchen. Her green eyes narrowed appraisingly. "Better on you than on me, as a matter of fact." Sarah had chosen a pale blue blouse, perhaps only a size too big. It must have been skintight on Melanie. A wraparound skirt in a blue calico print would have fit nearly anyone, but it did seem to hang perfectly over Sarah's slim hips. The white sandals were simple flats, two pieces of soft, buttery leather crossed over the vamp. As Melanie had predicted, it was barely noticeable that they were two sizes too large.

Melanie turned on the radio as she waited for the coffee to brew. That spared them any further attempts at conversation. Galveston had hardly escaped unscathed, and, of course, the storm had still not come as close as it was going to. Melanie's windows were tightly shuttered. Sarah got up and opened the kitchen door. The rain was coming down in sheets. The palm trees still bent nearly double in the wind. Had they rejoiced too soon? No, this still had to be better than a direct hit.

Sarah wondered about the rig. They wouldn't find out about that by listening to the radio. They wouldn't know until they could go out in the *Esmerelda,* and that would have to wait until the seas settled down to something approaching normal. That could be two or three days from now. She wondered how Ian would be able to stand the strain, when she was already nearly trembling with concern.

*   *   *

Melanie finally opened a conversation again as they were driving through the torrential rain toward the office. "Somehow you don't seem like his type."

Sarah thought carefully about her response and then decided to be honest. "Perhaps I'm not."

"What I meant was—"

"I know what you meant. What *I* meant is that neither Ian nor I knows yet whether we're each other's type. We don't always get along very well. I've never met anyone quite like him, and I don't think he's ever met anyone quite like me, either. At the moment I suspect that I'm a novelty to him. Novelties can wear off."

Melanie's eyes narrowed. "You sound as if you hope that you're more than a novelty."

"I don't know what I hope, Melanie," Sarah retorted in exasperation. "Don't ask now. And if you're smart, you won't ask him, either."

She could almost swear that Melanie purred in reply. "Don't you worry, honey. I know exactly what to ask Ian and what not to ask him. We Southern gals are taught early on how to please our men—and that includes providing a fair amount of novelty ourselves, if you get what I mean. I'm not out of this battle yet. There have been lots of women for Ian, but he's always come back to me."

Sarah blushed furiously. That was certainly

laying it on the line! She turned her head to stare out the window, concentrating on searching out the damage done by the storm.

When they arrived at the office, Ian greeted them cheerfully. "Well, how are my two favorite women this morning?" he asked. "Put the coffee on, Melanie, will you?"

Sarah raged inwardly. His two favorite women, indeed! She wondered if Melanie's thoughts toward him at that moment were as dark as her own.

Chapter Four

*T*HE radio spewed out its constant storm reports in the background as Ian and Sarah attacked the mountains of paperwork. He was certainly right that either he or someone else was needed in the office. It was obvious, however little Sarah might like to admit it, that Melanie did her best to keep up with it. The things that needed to be done were well organized—it was simply that they awaited the boss's approval, or the boss's directions, or the boss's presence. Melanie could scarcely schedule a necessary conference when Ian was still tied up on the rig. She could scarcely return a telephone call to the main MacDonald field when the foreman there had specifically asked to speak to Ian. But she had made lists of things that needed to be done and had even arranged them in what she felt to be the order of priority.

Sarah and Ian attacked the lists together. They found that there were some items she could handle and others that she could at least work through to some preliminary conclusion.

She felt more useful than she had since she'd arrived here. She was new in the field, but she had lots of experience at the types of things that they were slogging through today.

They looked up at ten-thirty in surprise as Melanie appeared with two steaming mugs of coffee. "Take a break, guys," she said pleasantly. "You haven't looked up from that mountain of stuff all morning. Go listen to the radio for a while or you'll be completely exhausted by noon."

Ian stood up and stretched. "Good thing Mellie takes such good care of me," he said.

In all sorts of ways, Sarah thought, gripping her coffee mug a little more tightly. She followed Ian into the outer office. She took one of the overstuffed chairs, carefully avoiding the sofa with its reminders of the previous night.

The storm was now just about fifteen miles off the coast—only ten miles or so from the rig. The waves were sweeping over the seawall at the northeastern end of the island. Sarah assumed that her motel and condominium were at least still standing, since there were no reports of any extensive damage.

She turned to Ian in consternation. "There's no report from your end of the island."

"There won't be," he said, "until the storm has passed. Then the Coast Guard helicopters will be up, and we'll get a pretty full report.

If we're lucky, they'll mention the rig as well—whether it's standing or whether it's down. But if there's a lot of other damage, the rig will be the furthest thing from their minds. Then we won't know one way or the other until we can take the *Esmerelda* out."

"And when might that be?"

"I wouldn't even expect the helicopters to be up until tomorrow morning. Let's not even think about the next step until then."

They finished their coffee in silence and returned to the paperwork. Melanie appeared solicitously again at around twelve-thirty. "Isn't anybody else hungry?"

"What's it like outside now, Mellie?" he asked.

"Still bad, according to the radio."

"Do you think we can find anything open?"

"The report says that most of the restaurants are closed. One supermarket is open, but it's supposed to be just for emergencies. Are we an emergency?"

"Unless there's any food at your place, we are."

Melanie thought hard. "Grilled-cheese sandwiches? Soup? That's probably about all I could manage. I wasn't really expecting company for lunch."

"Bless you, Melanie," he said.

At that moment even Sarah had to agree.

"We'll be here for supper, too, you know," Ian said later as he wolfed down the last sandwich. "Does that mean we have to hit the emergency supermarket on the way back to the office?"

Melanie seemed resigned to the situation. It hadn't yet been mentioned, but they all knew that Sarah would once again be bunking on her couch. She sighed. "No, there are some steaks in the freezer. You know, Ian, that I always try to be prepared for guests."

Sarah could almost see her thoughts as she looked up to meet Melanie's baleful green eyes—prepared for *one* guest, but not exactly pleased at the thought of two.

Melanie headed to the freezer to take out the steaks.

By five o'clock the stack of paperwork had been cut in half. "See," Sarah said in delight, "you don't have to spend all your time in the office. We'll have this out of the way by tomorrow. If we both spent two days a month in here, we could keep up with it."

Melanie walked in in time to catch the last part of that statement. "Not really," she said with a smug smile. "The stack that you two have been working on is only the most urgent pile. There are still mountains of work to catch up on." Ian and Sarah groaned, and Melanie continued. "It will be so nice to have you here full time, Ian. That's what this place really needs."

The unlikely trio lingered at the table over a bottle of wine, still listening to the storm report. Finally they headed to the living room for more of the same, this time on television. Sarah gasped as she saw, for the first time, the waves smashing over the seawall at her end of the island.

Trees lay strewn across the roads, and some beach buildings—bathhouses, food concessions—had been tossed to new spots on the beach. But all of the more substantial structures seemed to be intact. There had been no casualties, at least that anyone knew of. Property damage seemed extensive, despite the protection of the storm shutters. Cars had been crushed by falling trees, shingles had blown off roofs, landscaping was in a shambles.

They watched for about an hour in horrified fascination. Then Ian stood up and announced that he was going back to the office for the night. "Stay here," Melanie suggested, though she must have known what he would say. "There's the double bed in my room and the sofa here. We can manage to sleep three."

Sarah was relieved when Ian answered, "Thanks anyway, Mellie. But three's a crowd even under the best of circumstances . . . and it's certain that what we have here is far from the best of circumstances."

Ian's two "favorite women" reported to work promptly at eight the next morning, Sarah once again dressed in Melanie's clothes. At least, she thought, she had a sizable wardrobe to choose from. It wasn't exactly like being stranded on a desert island.

Melanie had brought her TV set into the office, knowing that if the helicopters went up, Ian would want to see for himself any scenes from the southwest end of the island or, with real luck, of the rig. She promised to stay glued to the screen and to shout to the two engineers if there was anything they wouldn't want to miss.

"They're clearing away the debris from the northeast end," she came in once to report. "The waves have receded to just below the top of the seawall. There's still a lot of flooding, but they expect to let people return to their homes by sometime tomorrow." She shot a glance at Sarah. *One more night,* they were both thinking.

"Ian, Ian, come quick," Melanie yelled in to them a little later. They dropped their reports and ran to the outer office, just in time to see a sweeping view of the island's southwest end. A solid sheet of water swept from the Gulf to the bay, but the houses seemed to be properly rooted rather than floating aimlessly about. "I may be home in a day or two also," Ian said hopefully.

Sarah and Ian worked cheerfully and efficiently, buoyed by the relatively good news that was coming their way. It was just before five that Melanie appeared at their door, looking stricken. "What is it, Mellie?" Ian asked.

"Some pieces of an oil rig have washed ashore," she said carefully, watching Ian as she spoke. He put his head down on his desk in despair as the two women stood by helplessly.

"Want to go back to my place for dinner?" Melanie asked, trying to change the subject. "There are more steaks in the freezer. I can thaw them in a few minutes in the microwave."

Ian got to his feet, shaking his head. "You and Sarah have them. I just want to be alone." He walked out of the office without another word.

Sarah and Melanie exchanged looks, sighed, and went back to Melanie's place, where they spent a silent, gloomy evening.

The next morning, though, Sarah noted that Melanie looked almost cheerful as they drove to work. Of course she would be happy to be seeing the last of her uninvited houseguest. Sarah wondered in what sort of shape they would find Ian.

Melanie paused before opening the car door when they arrived at the MacDonald offices. For just a moment she seemed at a loss for words. Then she said, all in a rush, "I want you to know that I think that you're not really such a bad sort. I'm not pleased that you're the competition, but other than that, you're okay."

"Thanks," Sarah said. "You're okay too. Thanks for everything, Melanie." Sarah knew that they might never be the best of friends, but the fact that they had just weathered a traumatic few days together had forged some sort of bond. That was what had happened between her and Ian, she realized. The traumatic experience had created a bond. It had been nothing more than that. She had to stop fantasizing about what might be. By next week he would be back to concentrating on Melanie. She had been warned.

They found Ian sound asleep on the couch in the outer office. Obviously he had had a few drinks too many the night before. Even asleep he looked wretched, with dark circles under his eyes and a stubbly growth of blond beard. They knew that he would look even worse awake, and so they tiptoed around him and left him lying there. Sarah went into his private office and once again attacked the paperwork.

She couldn't have been working for more than an hour when a big, booming voice made someone's presence known. She raced into the outer office to join with Melanie in trying to shush the owner of the noise. "Come on, Pete," she said, "let him sleep. He needs it."

Too late. Ian opened one bloodshot eye to gaze balefully at the foreman of his building crew. "Hung over, heh?" Pete bellowed. " 'Spected that. Well, pull yourself together, man. Let's take the *Esmerelda* out and see what's what."

"Leave me alone, Pete," Ian said. "We already know what's what. The pieces are washing ashore. The seas are still too rough for the launch, so we can't even get a salvage crew out there at least till tomorrow. I'll pull myself together by then." He turned over as if to dismiss them all.

Pete leaned over and shook his shoulder roughly. "So some pieces washed ashore. Big deal! If we're lucky, just the top section. I say we go out and see what's what. I can handle the *Esmerelda* in this sea. You coming, or aincha?"

Ian sat up and held his head. "I don't think that I could survive a trip on the *Esmerelda* today. As you've noticed, I'm not at my best."

"Fresh sea air'll fix you right up," Pete boomed. "Go wash your face, and we'll be off. Coming, Sarah?"

"You bet, Pete," she said with a grin.

"Somebody has to go along and hold his head while you steer the boat."

She should have vetoed this trip for both Ian and herself, Sarah thought as the little boat rose over the peaks and then down into the troughs of the choppy waves. Ian was a delightful shade of green. She felt as if she must be the same color, and that was even without a hangover. Only Pete was his usual smiling self, seemingly enjoying battling the heavy seas in the small boat.

It took well over an hour before the platform came into sight. She nudged Ian, who sat despondently with his head in his hands. He looked up and then did a double take. Pete had been right. The top section, the one that they had been working on before the storm had struck, was gone—sheared off cleanly, as if it had never been. But the rest of the derrick stood there in all its glory. Ian's face cleared as if someone had waved a magic wand. His baby was safe!

They climbed the platform—Sarah a little awkwardly in Melanie's skirt instead of her usual coveralls—and made a cursory inspection. They couldn't believe their good fortune. Three days' work had been wiped out when the top section of the derrick was lost, but they had to count that as minimal damage. "Should be able to get the crew out here tomorrow, boss," Pete yelled over the noise of the pounding waves. "You want 'em to work overtime to get back on schedule?"

"No . . . yes. Maybe a couple of hours a day, if they're willing, and the weekend too. That would get us right back on schedule by the end of next week."

Sarah saw Ian's shoulders sag. *The strain is over,* she thought. *He can relax now.*

"Shucks, Pete," he said, taking a deep breath, "I thought we were really wiped out this time."

Pete clapped him on the shoulder. "With the MacDonald luck? C'mon, man. A MacDonald's never lost a well!"

A MacDonald's never had a woman on a rig before, either, Sarah realized. If this rig had been destroyed, Ian would surely have remembered that his father had always insisted that a woman on a rig was like a woman on a ship— nothing but bad luck.

It was good to be back to strenuous physical activity. The men seemed to be working at peak efficiency as they struggled to rebuild the part of the derrick that had been destroyed. Ian and Sarah worked along with them, pitching in during the ten-hour shifts to try to get the building phase back on schedule.

Sarah's muscles ached at the end of each day. She would have enjoyed a before-dinner swim in the still-rough Gulf, but she arrived home so late that she was happy to settle for a fast-food meal, a long shower, and a soft bed. She wondered if Ian was spending his evenings with Melanie. Somehow she didn't think so. He must be as exhausted as she was. Melanie would probably have to wait until next week— or maybe even the week after that.

Ian approached Sarah as she walked to her car at the end of the long day on Sunday. "Going to stop for a burger, Sarah?" he asked. "I'll join you, if you don't mind."

In minutes they were at the restaurant. "We're back on schedule, you know," Ian said as they sat down with their burgers and fries. "You've been a big help—both on the rig and during those couple of days in the office. Sooner or later, Sarah, I'm going to be forced to admit that I'm glad I hired you."

She wondered again how he would have felt if the hurricane had destroyed the rig. "I'm glad we're back on schedule," she said non-committally.

"That means that you're in charge as of to-morrow," he continued. "This week I'll be right behind you. Next week, if all goes well, you're on your own."

She nodded. This had all been part of the

plan, and she was ready to face up to it. She tried not to think back to those two days in the office when, for the first time since she'd left New Jersey, she felt as if she knew exactly what she was doing. Learning new techniques was invigorating. Learning a new job was a challenge. She would have to keep telling herself that during the next week.

She didn't expect him to invite himself back to her motel room, and he didn't. She drove him back to the dock to reclaim his pickup and headed home for her shower and bed.

The next week was the worst of Sarah's life. Ian put her in charge of the crew, but he watched over her shoulder every minute. She knew that this was a necessary step, but that didn't make her like it any better. Each day Ian was professionally, chillingly polite to her on the rig; each evening he called her to read her a list of mistakes that she had made during the day.

"I'd rather be criticized on the spot," she protested finally.

"But that's not possible, Sarah. You know I want the men to feel that I have absolute confidence in you. Most of them share my qualms about having a woman on the rig. I've got to convince them that I've changed my attitude. I can't do that if I'm constantly criticizing you.

But I've got to get you in shape by the end of the week."

Sarah appreciated his logic, warped though it might be. "I'd hoped," she said sadly, "that I might have actually changed your attitude—at least a little bit."

"We've been over all this before, Sarah. I know you're smart. I know that you've got the stamina that fieldwork requires. I know that if you run across a valve that's too tough for you to turn, you feel comfortable about asking for help, and it's obvious to everybody—because it's obvious to you—that that's no reflection on your worth as an engineer. It's not as bad as I thought it would be—I'll grant you that." Almost as if he had caught himself mellowing, he reverted to a bellow. "But I'd still feel a lot more comfortable leaving a man in charge! What if you go to pieces in an emergency? What if you're daydreaming at a crucial time?"

Sarah found that insulting and made no secret of it. "That's nonsense, Ian. Why should I go to pieces in an emergency any more than you would? Why would I daydream on the job any more than a man would?"

He sounded almost apologetic. "All right, all right. Granted that I have enough faith in you to realize that. What if the men are really not as confident as they appear? Suppose that they've been putting on the same sort of good act for me that I've been putting on for them? Suppose that when I leave, they get nervous? Have you ever worked with a bunch of jumpy guys on a rig?''

"Ian, calm down." Sarah actually felt sorry for him. He was leaving her in charge of his baby, despite all his misgivings. "I'll let you know if there are problems. You're right; it's possible that it won't work out. The men may not accept me. There are some old guys on the crew who are probably even more set in their ways than you are—if that's possible—and some young ones who look at me as if they'd rather date me than take orders from me. But *I'll let you know.* You're not going to the other end of the earth. You'll be right in the onshore office."

She added the clincher, which she knew was a bald-faced lie: "I'd have no more hesitation in telling you that I couldn't handle the job than I would in asking one of the guys to open a valve for me."

On Friday, his last day on the rig, Ian was as jumpy as a cat. Sarah realized that if this was any indication of what the entire crew might be like on Monday, she would really have her work cut out for her. Maybe it had been a mistake. Ian's nervousness was rubbing off on her, and she knew that she couldn't command the respect of the men if she lost her air of authority. Rats! If she began to accept the MacDonald clan's opinion of the value of women on a rig, she might as well pack up and go back to New Jersey.

The weekend promised some interesting diversion. Friday night there was a party at Ian's house—the crew and their wives or dates—ostensibly to celebrate Sarah's takeover and Ian's return to the office. Sarah looked forward to noting any comments made after everyone had had a few drinks; she should be able to get a good idea of what lay in store for her on Monday.

Saturday would, at last, be a real change from the two weeks that she had so far been in Galveston. She had been spending nearly every waking moment, either on or off the job, with Ian. On Saturday, though, she was to move into her apartment. The movers would be arriving early in the morning with her share of the furniture from the apartment she had shared with Barbara. It was a rather lopsided collection—end tables but no sofa, china but no crystal, silver but no pots and pans.

She really would have to do some shopping soon to fill in the gaps. At least both she and Barbara had complete bedroom suites, and the dining-room table had belonged to Sarah. She could survive at least until the next weekend, when perhaps she could get into Houston and do some serious shopping.

She was really looking forward to settling into the apartment. It would be nice to get to know some people who had nothing to do with MacDonald Oil. With some luck there might even be some men who didn't have such strong feelings about professional women—some transplanted Northerners, perhaps.

Sarah dressed carefully on Friday night. Ian had told her to dress casually, but she knew that she wanted to look as enticing as Melanie. She had settled, finally, on black silk slacks with a matching camisole. With three-inch heels, she decided that she actually looked both tall enough and sophisticated enough—tall enough and sophisticated enough for *what* was not a question she cared to try to answer.

At Ian's house Melanie answered the door wearing skimpy shorts and a halter top. She looked Sarah up and down appraisingly, but said nothing. Sarah suddenly wondered if her outfit was all wrong. She followed Melanie through the empty living room toward the deck.

Ian detached himself from a small group and made his way over to Sarah. He kissed her primly on the cheek, but his intake of breath made it obvious to Sarah that he was not, tonight, seeing her as a business associate. "Well, Sarah," he said, "you look quite grown-up tonight."

He did hand out compliments in the strangest way! Sarah couldn't suppress a laugh. He took her arm and led her over to the people he had been talking with. Sarah noticed Melanie's scowl and subtly detached herself from his grip. She didn't care what Melanie thought, but Melanie's look had reminded her that she didn't want the rest of the group to get any mistaken ideas about her relationship with Ian.

Melanie wandered over to them, an expression of almost overdone innocence on her face. "I'll introduce Sarah to everyone, Ian," she said.

"Thanks, Melanie," he said offhandedly.

Melanie took Sarah in tow, making sure that she met the crew members on the midnight shift as well as the wives or girlfriends of those whom she already knew. Sarah tried hard to concentrate on the introductions, but she was fighting a feeling of growing annoyance. She admitted that Melanie was behaving very properly. Why, then, did she find herself so distressed?

Someone got Sarah a drink, and she soon was caught up in a group discussing the attractions—and lack thereof—of the city of

Galveston. Sarah was, of course, very interested in what they had to say. After all, she had
just contracted to spend three years of her life
in this city. Between the discussion and the
spectacular sunset over the water, she was suf-
ficiently distracted to forget her annoyance at
Melanie—until she ambled over with a tray of
hors d'oeuvres. It was then that Sarah realized
what was bothering her. Melanie was playing
the role of hostess.

Of course, Sarah told herself. *Of course
Melanie would be the hostess.* And what difference did it make, anyway? It was not as if *she*
wanted the job of passing the hors d'oeuvres.

Sarah tried not to keep glancing around toward Melanie or Ian, but it was hard to resist.
The gorgeous receptionist spent most of the
evening hanging onto her boss, who didn't look
as if he minded very much.

It was only ten-thirty. Sarah could hardly
leave, and yet she was really not enjoying the
party. Finally she could stand it no longer. She
found Ian, still quite literally wrapped up in
Melanie, and made her excuses. "I'm sorry to
even think of leaving so early," she explained,
"but I've got a splitting headache. I guess all
the events of the past couple of weeks are finally catching up to me. Thank you, Ian. I had
a lovely time. I'll see you on Monday. Good
night, Melanie."

Melanie smiled smugly as she wished Sarah good night, but the smile turned to a frown as Ian detached himself from her. "Wait a minute, Sarah," he said. "It's really too early to call it a night. Come for a walk on the beach with me. Getting away from the crowd and out into the fresh air should clear your head. Melanie will take care of the guests for me while I'm gone. Won't you, Melanie?"

Melanie was glaring at Sarah as if she had other ideas on how to take care of her head. Sarah couldn't resist. "That's very sweet of you, Ian," she said, smiling up at him. "Maybe it would help. I'd love to find that I didn't have to leave quite yet, after all." She felt as if a thousand knives were being directed at her as she turned her back on Melanie and left with Ian.

Sarah took off her high heels and carried them as they walked along in the soft sand. She looked longingly at the soft waves rolling in to shore. One of these days, she thought, she must find some time for another swim. Her headache was receding. Ian had been mercifully quiet; they walked along in comfortable silence.

She was the one to speak first. "Thanks, Ian. My head feels much better. We can get back to your guests now."

"Don't worry about the guests," he said.

"Melanie can handle them. I've been wanting some time with you all evening, but I couldn't seem to shake loose."

"I noticed that."

"Melanie is a little possessive," he said ruefully.

"And I'm sure that you haven't given her any reason to feel possessive," she countered sarcastically.

He successfully ignored her comment by taking her into his arms. She recognized that this was what she had been waiting for all evening, and the last of her tension evaporated as she lost herself in his kiss.

"Ian," came the shout from just a short distance away. "Ian, Sarah . . . where are you?"

He muttered an oath under his breath.

"Oh, there you are," Melanie said innocently as she approached. "Some of your guests are starting to leave, Ian, and I just knew that you'd want to say good night to them."

Ian said something unintelligible, then took a deep breath. "Sure, Melanie. Thanks for calling us. I didn't realize that it was getting so late." He took Sarah's hand as he headed back to the house. Melanie ignored that and latched on to his other arm. *We look like the three musketeers,* Sarah thought as they strolled back along the sand.

Sarah left Ian to Melanie when they got back

to the house. There seemed to be no point in indulging in a public contest for Ian's attentions. She concentrated on trying to overhear small comments that might indicate problems she would be having with the men, but no one seemed in a grousing mood. For an entirely different set of reasons than previously, she still couldn't really get into the swing of things.

She made a feeble attempt for another hour or so. There was no point in having the entire crew think that she was standoffish—Monday would bring her enough problems without that—but before too long she was once again making her excuses and saying good night to Ian. He looked at her searchingly, with Melanie still clinging to his side. Then, miraculously enough, he said, "Excuse me, Melanie," and walked Sarah to her car.

"We've got to talk, Sarah," he said. "I know that your movers are coming tomorrow; I'll come over and help you rearrange furniture and unpack cartons. I probably won't be there till around noon—heaven knows when this thing will break up tonight, so I don't want to make it any earlier." He kissed her gently and closed the car door after her. She looked up toward the house to see Melanie watching them from the doorway.

Chapter Five

S ARAH tossed and turned throughout the night. She was certain that she was a game to Ian—a female engineer, a puzzle. He wanted to know where the engineer left off and the female began. He would be proud of this conquest.

No doubt she should refuse to play the game. She knew that she had nothing to gain. Ian would never be hers. She was surely just an interesting experiment. And what if she could actually win him? Was she ready to give up her career and become the mother of a large brood of children? She honestly didn't know.

The movers arrived at nine the next morning. By the time Ian showed up at noon, Sarah had most of her few belongings unpacked.

"You look tired, Sarah," he said. "You've really been working too hard since you've been here. I'm sorry I couldn't get here earlier this morning to help you, but the party didn't break up until three."

And then there was undoubtedly Melanie, Sarah thought. The thought riled her, and she snapped at him. "You didn't exactly leave me relaxed and ready to drop off to sleep last night."

He grinned and reached out for her hand. "That's nice to know. It would be terrible to feel that I'd had no effect on you whatsoever. Come on—since I'm too late to help with the unpacking, I'll at least take you out to lunch."

Sarah hesitated. Things were squared away much earlier than she had anticipated. She had the whole afternoon—perhaps she should use it to do some shopping. "Ian," she said, "I appreciate the offer. But what I really should do is get myself into Houston. As you can see, my belongings do a nice job of semifurnishing an apartment. I'd really like to at least get some pots and pans so I can do some cooking."

"Do female engineers do things like that?" he quipped. She ignored the comment, and he continued. "Well, if that's the agenda for the day, it's all right with me. Since I've scheduled you into my afternoon, I'll go with you and help you shop. Actually, there are several good shopping malls on Galveston Island; I'm not trying to duck out of a drive to Houston, but I think you should see what the locals have to offer first. We should at least find some pots and pans.

"I'd demand a sample of your cooking in exchange for my efforts, but I think that after an afternoon's shopping you'll be in no shape to show off your culinary prowess. Maybe we can stop on the way home for a bottle of wine and some Mexican food to bring back here and at least celebrate by having dinner in your new apartment."

If only it could go on like this, she thought. Here he was, being the epitome of helpfulness and courtesy. Then she reminded herself that this was just the good side of the proper Southern gentleman's behavior toward women. Helping the little lady settle into an apartment was one thing; letting the little lady on your oil rig was quite another. Oh, well. Sarah sighed inwardly. Might as well relax and enjoy the good parts, since she sure couldn't avoid the bad.

They stopped for a quick lunch at an oyster bar and then headed to the center of Galveston for the first stage of their trek. Sarah was pleasantly surprised at the variety and quality of the shops, being forced to admit that it was possible to find almost anything one might want without, as she had anticipated, making a trip clear to New York. Some French copper cookware was her first purchase. She was so pleased that she volunteered to cook dinner that night, after all, but Ian firmly vetoed the suggestion.

"You're dead on your feet and just don't

know it yet, Sarah," he predicted. "You're going to collapse when I get you home."

Sarah protested, they argued laughingly, and then they reached a compromise—he would come back for her home-cooked dinner on Sunday night. With that settled, she realized that grocery shopping should be next—and the very thought made her realize that he was exactly right about how tired she was. Looking for a sofa would simply have to wait until another day.

It was when they stopped for the wine that Sarah realized that at least one more purchase was necessary—she had no wine glasses. "We've got to go back to the center of town," she moaned. "I don't mind drinking wine out of jelly glasses, but I don't even have any jelly glasses."

Back they went. Sarah settled quickly on a Waterford pattern that she'd long admired and splurged on six wine goblets, commenting jokingly that she'd just spent her first paycheck and that these would have to do for orange juice, milk, and water until she saved enough money to complete the set—or enough jelly glasses so that she wouldn't have to.

Sarah was really glad that Ian had won the argument over the take-home food. It took all of her remaining effort to set the table. Dinner did revive her somewhat, though. If she had a couch and some chairs, she thought, and if her stereo were hooked up, they would have a pleasant evening ahead of them.

Ian caught her look and headed toward an unpacked carton. She looked at him quizzically. "Deck chairs," he said. "The label says there are deck chairs in here."

He was right. Sarah had forgotten about the deck chairs; forgotten, even, about the deck. In a few minutes Ian had set up a cozy arrangement. He poured some more wine, and they relaxed in silence.

"Sarah," he said finally, "I apologize for leaning so hard on you this week."

She was too tired to get into another argument. "I understand," she said and was surprised to realize that she *did* understand. She might not agree, but she did understand.

"Thanks," he said as he stood up. "Bedtime, Sarah," he said. He took her by the hand and pulled her to her feet. "You've had a busy day. I'll see you tomorrow around six. Now get some sleep." He kissed her gently and left.

Sarah woke early, feeling fully rested and eager for the evening with Ian. She did some preliminary preparations for dinner—a chicken dish that was one of her specialties— put a bottle of wine into the refrigerator to chill, and went off in search of a Sunday newspaper and some donuts for breakfast. She read the paper on the deck, then came in and baked a pie for dessert. Chicken and apple pie—that should convince him he'd found a girl just like Mom! Of course, on the following day he would be once again criticizing her engineering decisions. . . .

By midafternoon there were only last-minute details left to accomplish, and Sarah put on her bathing suit and headed out for her long-awaited swim. It was nice to be able to walk out the front door and be on the beach. Aside from her professional relationship with her boss, Sarah had no regrets over leaving the New York area. Looking from her deck out over the Gulf of Mexico was every bit as breathtaking as looking out toward the Manhattan skyline.

When he arrived that evening, Ian brought flowers and another bottle of wine—the Southern gallantry again. He raved over Sarah's cooking and surprised her by helping clear the dishes from the table.

"I didn't think that Southern gentlemen did things like that, Ian," she couldn't resist commenting.

"Good thing this is a luxury apartment—with a dishwasher!" he countered. "There are limits to the compromises we male chauvinists are prepared to make."

They retreated to the deck again after dinner. Again they sat in silence, but this time Sarah found the silence strained.

Ian came over and pulled her to her feet. He held her close and kissed her, tenderly at first, and then with greater insistence. She stiffened. "What's the matter, Sarah?" he whispered.

"I—I don't know."

He led her back into the living room, still nearly bare except for the dining table and chairs. He switched on the stereo, commenting that it was obvious she hadn't needed to wait for any clever male to set it up, and took her in his arms and began to dance.

Sarah relaxed, lost in that wondrous feeling of being in his arms. Gradually he held her tighter, so gradually she forgot to be frightened, forgot that they were probably engaged in a contest that would have no real winner.

"It's not a contest, Sarah," he whispered, as if he had read her mind. "You don't have to prove anything to me."

"Is it that obvious?" she asked, feeling close to tears.

He kissed her gently—lips, eyelids, nose, lips again. "Yes, Sarah. It's that obvious. You spend your days trying to impress me, and now you feel you have to impress me in the evenings as well. Forget it, Sarah. Forget everything and just enjoy."

*   *   *

Sarah awoke to an alarm that she didn't remember setting. She smiled contentedly, feeling rested for the first time in weeks.

She showered and fixed some breakfast. The reality of the day was sinking in. It was Monday, and in just a little over an hour she would be completely in charge of an oil rig. It was a sobering thought—sobering enough to put last night's fairy tale right out of her mind.

Later, on the job, Sarah wondered if she was imagining the sullen looks as she climbed the ladder to the rig. Ian had allowed her to issue most of the orders during the last week, but she had always known that she had him standing with her for support. Never had she felt so alone as she did at this moment. Suppose something went wrong? There were a million things that might go wrong even if Ian were here and she were not, but if something happened while she was in charge, she knew it would confirm all of his feelings about female engineers. She took a deep breath to chase the goblins away.

The well was not yet at a critical stage. They should be ready to start drilling by the beginning of the following week, and the best estimates were that they were unlikely to hit pay dirt for at least three to four weeks after that. Ian had promised to be back on board in just under a month so he could monitor the final stages of the drilling.

All Sarah had to do, she reminded herself, was to finish the final checkout, begin the drilling, and keep things running smoothly. It was all routine. There was no reason to be nervous. The men were as anxious to bring in this well as she was. Surely they would continue to work like the well-functioning team that she knew they were.

By the end of the first day she was exhausted. How, she wondered, could it be ten times as hard when Ian wasn't there? Ian . . . she realized that she hadn't spared a thought for him since she climbed the ladder at eight A.M. Well, he would have been proud of her today. She was pretty certain that a few of the men had been grumbling behind her back, but there had been no snide comments made openly. They were all accepting her orders as if they had been given by Ian himself. The checkout was proceeding on schedule, despite one malfunctioning pump that had been replaced. It had been a textbook day—but exhilarating in a way that would be impossible to imagine if one had only read about it.

Sarah shook out her hair as she removed her hard hat after settling in the launch for the trip back to port. She thought of the old TV commercial and of Barbara's comments and chuckled inwardly. Barbara was right. That girl must have been as exhausted and sweaty as Sarah now was and couldn't possibly have been ready for a night of dancing.

She stopped on the way home for a fast-food burger. Despite all those lovely new pots and pans, she knew that she was too tired to cook. By eight o'clock she was fast asleep.

Tuesday was somewhat easier. The nervousness was gone, and with it the resulting strain that had made the first day so exhausting. The work continued on schedule, and Sarah's confidence returned, though she was still aware of some secretive comments from the men. She was anxious to tell Ian how well it was going.

She broiled herself some lamb chops and tossed a salad. Tonight she was awake enough to wonder why Ian hadn't called. She wondered if she should call him; after all, she could reasonably be expected to report to her supervisor periodically. She imagined him in Melanie's welcoming arms. She wondered what Melanie knew that she didn't about keeping a man like Ian happy. She could have been eating broiled hockey puck instead of five dollars' worth of lamb chops, for all the notice she took of what she was chewing.

The phone made her jump. She took a deep breath and counted to ten before answering; it wouldn't do to have him know that she'd been sitting right next to it.

"How is it going?" he asked.

It was amazing how happy she was to hear even such a mundane question. "Fine," she assured him. "We had to replace the number-three pump yesterday, but it's been repaired and is ready to be used again if need be. Aside from that, everything is proceeding as expected. We'll be ready to start drilling on Monday if there are no serious hitches. Actually, we could probably be ready on Friday, but I'd prefer to take my time and do one more dry run."

He grunted approvingly. "I've scheduled the drilling crew to arrive on Monday, anyway."

"The drilling crew?" Sarah could scarcely believe her ears. She cursed herself for betraying the fact that she hadn't known that another crew would be arriving.

"Surely I've mentioned . . . certainly you didn't think. . . . No matter. The building crew will begin working on Rig Number Two. That's a bit of a problem—it means a large investment before we've established a proven field.

"But the alternative is to send them back to the MacDonald field in the northern part of the state, and then they'd probably be involved in building a rig there just when we wanted them.

No, best to take a chance and get on with Number Two . . . and pray that Number One hits oil by the time that Number Two is finished. Then we'll be able to start the building crew on the permanent platform, which will service six or seven more wells. Otherwise. . . ." His voice trailed off.

Sarah realized that he had been talking to himself as much as to her. It was just as well, since her own thoughts were racing. Another crew to try to win over!

"Any problems with the men?" he asked, almost as if reading her mind.

"I don't think so. There's a little muttering among them when they think I'm out of earshot, but I don't think it's anything serious. I didn't expect them to be jumping up and down for joy. After all, they're all Southern gentlemen."

He ignored the barb. "Are you sure you're okay? I could come back out for a day if you think it's necessary."

"Already that anxious to escape the office? Thanks, but I don't think it would be a good idea. The men have to be convinced that I know what I'm doing without having you check things out every step of the way."

"All right, Sarah. You're right, of course. It sounds as if you have things well in hand." Sarah could hear his intake of breath, and she could almost picture his effort to shift mental gears. "I guess that takes care of business. Now then . . . are you ready for a swim, or are you too tired?"

Her heart leaped. She felt almost physically ill as she forced herself to relax, realizing only now just how afraid she had been that he had called merely to find out about the well. "A swim sounds great," she managed to say. "A few minutes, then?"

She hung up the phone with trembling fingers. This might be a game to Ian, but it was no longer—and probably never had been—a game to Sarah. She faced the fact that she was in love with him. Now what? He'd be really pleased if he knew exactly how great his conquest was!

She took a deep breath to try to regain some of her equanimity. She would have to try not to behave like a college sophomore. It was obvious that Ian had been involved with lots of women, and none of them had become a permanent fixture in his life. She would try to follow his lead, enjoying the moment without thinking about the future.

It wasn't what Sarah had hoped for, a relationship without a sense of commitment—on both sides—but it was surely all that Ian was prepared to give her. Sarah knew with absolute certainty that she loved him enough to settle for whatever he was willing to give.

The swim was brief and invigorating, the good-night kiss the merest touch. But Sarah was optimistic again. He was no longer on *her* rig. Perhaps that really would make it possible for him to concentrate on her as a woman. She could make her daily report . . . they would shift gears. . . .

By Wednesday, as Sarah toyed with her food while waiting for Ian's phone call, her doubts were surfacing again. By the time the phone rang, she was once again convinced that she was only an experiment to him, a novelty that would soon grow stale.

"Everything okay?" he asked.

"Calm as can be."

"It still has to be more exciting than the office."

Even though Melanie is there, Sarah thought. That was encouraging. She tried unsuccessfully to think of something exciting to report. There was an awkward pause. Somehow she knew that he wouldn't suggest another swim. She forced herself to take the initiative. "Would you like to come over for a drink?"

"Not tonight, Sarah. I'll check back with you tomorrow to see how things are on the rig."

Not even a pretense of an explanation. Well,

she didn't own him. He didn't have to explain his schedule to her. Still, she had hoped. . . . Well, she told herself, it was time to stop hoping. For her this had always been a no-win situation—whether he decided that she was woman or engineer or some miraculous combination, he was obviously not falling desperately in love with her . . . as she was with him. Sarah cried herself to sleep.

Chapter Six

*S*ARAH woke up in the morning puffy-eyed and filled with determination. She wasn't the first woman to regret falling for someone who would never love her, and she wouldn't be the last. Others had managed to pick up the pieces, and she would too. She'd be ready to report to Ian on Friday, and periodically thereafter, but she would put him out of her mind aside from that. She would begin tonight, by going to the condo's game room after dinner. Meeting some other people would be good for her.

The rig was nearly ready for the drilling to begin. Sarah was becoming increasingly excited about that prospect, even though all her textbooks—and Ian—agreed that the drilling itself would probably take a matter of weeks.

Sarah thought again of the TV commercial as she took off her hard hat at the end of the day. Tonight she really was going partying. At the moment she was tired and sweaty, and, unlike the girl in the commercial, she planned to go home and shower, eat, and relax a bit before going out for the evening, but she still smiled to herself at the thought and wondered what Barbara would say.

The party room was crowded. The condominium was one that would be expected to appeal to young, affluent singles, and this was borne out by the group there tonight. Sarah was quickly made to feel at home. Several of the men spent the evening vying for her attention. Even more important, in Sarah's view—because they were harder for her to find—she met quite a few compatible women.

Sarah met a psychiatrist and a marine biologist, both, much to her surprise, real Southern belles. She looked forward to long chats with them about the problems between modern Southern women and old-fashioned Southern men. There was also a fair assortment of transplanted Northerners, both men and women. Sarah enjoyed comparing notes with them and realized by the end of the evening that not one of them had expressed any longing for their hometowns.

It was Paul who monopolized her time during the later part of the evening, and Paul who convinced her to have dinner with him Friday night. Paul was a resident surgeon at the University of Texas Medical Branch in Galveston. He was a Texas native but had gone to college in the East. Sarah would have gone out with him solely to check out his view on professional women, but, as it turned out, he was also witty and charming and a good dancer. All in all, there certainly seemed to be no reason to say no. Surely the expected call from Ian didn't leave her feeling compelled to sit waiting by the phone.

The rig was ready for Monday, and Sarah was in a mood for celebration when Paul picked her up on Friday night. He ushered her into a silver-gray Porsche—quite a change, Sarah noted, from Ian's pickup truck—and took her to a little restaurant in the historic district, where the Mexican food was authentic and delicious. They moved on to a nightclub on the bay for drinks and dancing and finished up with coffee back at the apartment.

Sarah had enjoyed herself immensely and had managed to more or less keep her mind off Ian. She barely hesitated when Paul suggested that they spend the day at Marine World the following day. Their evening finished with the lightest of good-night kisses, the barest hint of things to come.

They started out bright and early the next morning. Paul wore neither cowboy boots nor a western hat. Apparently his college years in the North had rubbed away most of his Texan mannerisms.

Sarah enjoyed this chance to play tourist;

she had really still seen very few of the sights. She cheered at the porpoise show and laughed at the seals as they clowned for the crowd. She gasped at the sharks and turned up her nose at the alligators. They fed the sea lions and relaxed at the water-skiing show at the end of the day. Sarah realized just what a different sort of Southern gentleman she had stumbled onto when he invited her to *his* apartment for dinner.

It was certainly not the chrome-and-plush bachelor pad that Sarah had expected, and she fell in love with it instantly. The living room was lined with bookshelves. The large doors to the deck, like hers, looked over the Gulf, where the sun was just beginning to set. Sarah plopped down into one of the overstuffed chairs, took off a sandal, and massaged an aching foot.

Paul put a Mozart sonata on the stereo, went to the kitchen, and returned with two glasses of wine. They spent the next half hour talking about their careers, their childhoods . . . all the things that new friends find to talk about. Paul refilled the glasses and invited her to join him in the kitchen.

It was apparent to Sarah that she was expected merely to serve as company; Paul obviously had the cooking well in hand. He tossed a beautiful spinach-and-mushroom salad while the broiler heated, plunked in two well-trimmed steaks and set the timer, and put another bottle of wine in the refrigerator to chill. Then he ushered her out to the deck to catch the last of the sunset.

Dinner was perfect. They lingered over coffee, hating to say good night but not wanting to rush things in this new and fragile relationship. Sarah finally pleaded exhaustion with utter truthfulness, and he walked her to the door of her apartment.

Sarah was awakened on Sunday morning by the shrill ringing of the telephone. "Where in the devil were you?" Ian demanded.

"Off duty, I thought," she replied testily.

He might not have heard her. "I expected a report on that well. I've been trying to reach you since Friday evening!"

"The well is ready to go. No hitches. Will that be all?" Her voice was icy.

He was obviously displeased by her tone. "Yes," he snapped. "For now, that's all. I'll call you again tomorrow night to see if the drilling got started all right."

"I may not be home," she countered.

"Sarah, I don't know what you're doing, and I don't care. But I would think that you would be in before the wee hours, at least. You can't direct that crew if you're exhausted or half asleep."

There was not much she could say to that; he was absolutely right. "You're right," she admitted. "If I do go out, I'm sure that I'll be home by ten."

"Good," he said smugly. "I'll be talking to you tomorrow night, then."

Sarah was shaking as she hung up the phone. Why, she wondered, did that man have such an effect on her? Furious though she may be, she knew that it would not take much for her to be back in his arms. The call had certainly put a damper on her anticipation of a pleasant day with Paul.

She brightened again when Paul arrived. He had a way of making her feel at ease. The relationship had none of the shooting stars that were there with Ian, but it had none of the more unpleasant fireworks, either.

Sarah and Paul spent the day on the beach. They ate dinner at her apartment and finished up the evening by pedaling a fringe-roofed surrey along the seawall. They both knew that the next day was a big one for Sarah, and it was barely ten o'clock as they said good night. Sarah recognized a stab of disappointment when he explained that he would be on night duty for the next week.

Sarah tossed and turned in bed. Part of her mind was on the well; she was nervous about the drilling, even though she told herself over and over again that everything had checked out perfectly. She was apprehensive about meeting the drilling crew. They were old hands at their job, and the drill chief had worked for Ian's dad since the early days. They might be even more reluctant to have her as the supervisor than the building crew had been.

She was disappointed over the fact that she wouldn't be seeing Paul for a week; they might not ever be more than good friends, but a good friend was exactly what she needed right now. She was angry at Ian. He seemed at times as if he felt about her as she felt about him. At other times he seemed to distance himself, defining his role as her supervisor. Even as her boss he seemed somewhat remiss; she could hardly believe that she was to greet the new crew without him there by her side. It felt like walking into a lion's den.

She missed Barbara. She really would have to make an effort to get to know some of the other women in the condo, though it would take a long time to become as close to someone new as she had been to Barbara. On impulse she picked up the phone and dialed the number of her old apartment.

Barbara answered sleepily. Delight was evident in her voice, even as she yelled, "Sarah, you kook, it's after midnight here. Don't you have to work in the morning?"

Sarah filled her in quickly—on the well, on Ian, on Paul, ending with a plaintive plea. "You're due for some vacation time, Barbara. Can't you fly out and stay for a week or so? I'll be working all day, of course, but the beach is just a few steps from my door. And we'd have the evenings, and the weekends. . . ."

"Actually," was the response, "I'd been thinking about that very thing. I had been dreaming of someplace exotic, but then I realized that I'd rather see you."

"Maybe you could have both," Sarah said. "Let me check into some weekend cruises or charter flights to the Yucatan."

After chatting with her old roommate for a while longer, Sarah felt better than she had since arriving in Galveston. She fell asleep quickly and awoke calm and filled with confidence as she faced her exciting day.

Ian *was* waiting at the launch when she arrived. He was coolly professional, but she was so happy to see him that she didn't mind. He introduced her to the men, fixing a baleful look on one whose face betrayed his feelings about having a female supervisor. "I expect you to treat Sarah exactly as you would treat me . . . or Dad," he cautioned.

He called Sarah aside in the last moments before it was time for the launch to be on its way. "Don't worry," he said comfortingly. "The drill boss, Mike Adams, is the best in the business. Never has there been a supervisory job with so little for the supervisor to do. Within a week or so you should be able to amuse yourself by visiting the Number Two Rig site occasionally. A casual keeping an eye on things is really all that's needed."

He made it all sound so easy. "I was hoping that you might be coming along today," she ventured.

"And mess up your chance to prove that you're as much of a man as I am?"

He laughed and waved good-bye. Sarah's eyes stung with tears.

The drilling was, as Ian had warned her, an anticlimax. The crew ran a final check, Mike Adams gave the order to begin, and the huge gears started in motion. The noise was unnerving, after the silence that had been the way of life on the rig since it was built. After an hour or so of monitoring the equipment, there was really nothing to do. Sarah wondered how the building crew was doing as they started Number Two Rig. She recalled that Ian was anxious to be on that rig and wondered if he had begun looking for a business manager.

Ian called at six that night. "I thought that this might be a reasonable time to catch you at home," he began. "How did it go?"

"No problems," Sarah answered. "It's actually kind of boring now that there's nothing left to do."

He grunted in response. "It sure is. That's why I was willing to get off and let you take over—not that this stupid office work is any better. It's getting 'em ready that's exciting—that and, of course, finally bringing in the oil. I wouldn't miss that part for anything. Well, good night now. I'll call occasionally to see how things are going, and I'll be back on the rig in three more weeks."

The week flew by, despite the boredom of the job and Paul's absence in the evenings. Sarah made one trip out to the site of Rig Number Two, but there really wasn't much to see at this stage of the game.

She managed to do a little shopping each night after work, and the apartment was beginning to look a little less as though she were camping out. She checked on dates of cruises to Mexico and fired off a letter to Barbara with dates and details. She spent a couple of hours before bed each evening in the party room, getting to know some more of her fellow tenants and strengthening the growing friendship that she had begun with some of the women.

On Saturday she went to several of the shopping malls in search of the last important item—a sofa. She was just coming out of one of Galveston's more exclusive furniture stores, still undecided over several sofas that she'd seen, when a familiar voice behind her said, "Why, Sarah honey, what a surprise to see you alone!"

Sarah turned to find herself face to face with Melanie, whose expression hardly matched her honey-dripping tone of voice. "And whom did you expect to find me with?" Sarah asked, wondering if Melanie had heard that she'd spent a lot of time out last weekend.

"Don't play Miss Innocent with me," Melanie sniped. "He was mine before you came along. I would have thought that you could have found your own man, without stealing one who was already spoken for."

Sarah looked perplexed. "I don't know what you're talking about, Melanie," she said, turning to go.

"I know that Ian's been spending every evening with you. Well, don't think that you're going to keep him. I'll get him back—you'll see." She turned and walked away, leaving Sarah standing openmouthed.

Sarah took a break from the shopping to have a cup of coffee and collect her thoughts. So Melanie thought that she was seeing Ian . . . and she had thought that Ian had gone running back to Melanie! It was really too much to figure out. Sarah had another cup of coffee and went back to the store to order a sofa.

Paul appeared at her doorstep Monday after work, bottle of wine in hand. "Your place or mine?" he quipped.

Sarah realized that she really should do a better job of keeping the refrigerator and freezer stocked for such eventualities. "I could scramble some eggs," she ventured.

"That settles it, then. I can do better than that." He took her arm and propelled her out the door toward the elevator.

She joined him in the kitchen while he skillfully assembled a meat pie. He put it into the oven and poured the drinks. "I hope that your week was less eventful than mine," he said once they were seated on the deck, again admiring the sunset. "Night duty is always rough. That's when most of the accident cases and all of the assault victims show up."

It was pleasant to be back with Paul again. Pleasant and relaxing. "My week was calm and boring," she said. "I thought that it would be more exciting to be drilling, but it's quite the opposite. The only exciting thing was that I talked my former roommate into spending some vacation time with me. We'll be trying to book a weekend cruise to Mexico. Oh—and I bought a sofa."

"Maybe next week you'll buy some groceries," he teased.

"Now that you mention it, I'll make a quick stop on my way home from work tomorrow night. I'll expect you at six-thirty for veal parmigiana."

The week continued in its uneventful way. Sarah and Paul continued to enjoy each other's company, but the relationship showed no signs of developing into a romance. For Sarah, that was perfect. She needed this time of uninvolvement, time to grow used to the fact that she couldn't have Ian. She wondered about the women in Paul's past, wondered if he, too, were recuperating from something painful. She was content to ask no questions, happy to have this delightful man as a companion.

Saturday morning brought a pounding on the door. She opened it in housecoat and slippers, hair in disarray, rubbing the sleep from her eyes. Ian stood there, looking, as usual, as if he were in a rage.

"Everything is fine, Ian," she said groggily. "I would have been glad to tell you that over the phone."

"I didn't come to check on the well," he

snapped. "I came because I couldn't stay away. I've tried, but it's not possible."

Sarah stared at him dumbfoundedly, then turned to the kitchen to put on a pot of coffee.

Chapter Seven

*S*ARAH got a good look at Ian while the coffee perked. He was unshaven and looked tired. "Have you eaten?" she asked. It was a strangely mundane question. This man had appeared at her doorstep and told her that he couldn't stay away from her, and she was brewing coffee and asking him if he'd had breakfast. She felt detached from the scene, as if she were viewing it from afar. Perhaps after she'd had her coffee. . . . She was never at her best first thing in the morning.

Ian sat on a stool at the kitchen counter. After his first outburst he had been silent, as if he, too, were having trouble marshaling his thoughts at this early hour. Sarah poured him a cup of coffee and went off to comb her hair and add a quick dash of lipstick. She returned and noncommittally began to scramble some eggs.

"This helps," he said finally after polishing off the eggs and toast and starting his third cup of coffee. "I guess I sounded a bit foolish, barging in here like that."

131

Sarah certainly didn't want him to think that anything he'd said was foolish! "I wasn't really quite awake, Ian. Why don't you run it all by me again?"

He approached it calmly this time. "I'm sorry I backed off from you with no explanation, Sarah. It was clear to me that an involvement with my second-in-command was a bad idea. I knew that some of the men weren't all that much in favor of you, and I knew that it was insanity to give them something to whisper about. I never meant to get involved with you; I was merely trying to be polite—show you around, things like that—to make up for being so rotten to you at first."

Sarah raised one eyebrow. "And, incidentally, to check out what a female engineer might be like off the job?"

"A bit of that too," he admitted offhandedly. "Anyway, I thought that I could take up where I left off with Melanie and forget all about you. But it hasn't worked out that way." He looked searchingly at her, and she flushed under his gaze. "You're beautiful in the morning, do you know that?"

"And now what? Nothing has changed. It's still insanity to be involved with your second-in-command. I still haven't won over all the men; in fact, I've made less progress with the new crew. What brings you here now?"

"I told you, Sarah, when you were too sleepy to know what I was saying. In my carefully rehearsed speech I told you that I can't stay away from you. Every time I call you for a report on the well, I spend the night tossing and turning because I want you to be more than my assistant. I don't know how we'll manage to handle the situation, but we've got to work it out somehow. I have to be with you, Sarah."

Not one word of love. He was inviting her to play a dangerous game with no long-term commitments.

"You're asking me to see you off the job but keep it a secret." She said it almost to herself. It was not phrased as a question.

Ian spread his hands in exasperation. "Sarah, I'd be proud to have the world know that I'm involved with you. It just somehow doesn't seem practical at the moment."

Somehow that was not what she had hoped for. What she had hoped for, she didn't know, but certainly not that. "Ian," she said slowly, trying to formulate her thoughts while she talked, "I don't think that I'm cut out for secretive relationships."

She could see the struggle of some decision in his eyes. He attempted a smile, not very successfully. "Let's just take it slowly, then. Though you've got reason enough to hate me,

I don't really think that you do. Will you have dinner with me tonight, Sarah?"

Sarah let out the breath that she had been holding. She still had a chance. "Yes, I'd like that, Ian," she managed to say.

"Good. Now pour me another cup of coffee and report on the rig." Sarah had to laugh as he propped his boot-clad foot on her kitchen chair and looked at her in his old chauvinistic way.

Ian was still there an hour later when Paul arrived at the door. "I know that we hadn't any plans for the day—" he began, then stopped as he saw Ian. "I'm sorry, Sarah. I didn't realize you had company."

"It's all right, Paul. It's my boss. Come on in, and I'll introduce you." She suddenly realized that she was still in her robe and added hastily, "He woke me bright and early this morning for a report on the rig."

She opened the door wider as an invitation to Paul, but he declined. "I won't disturb you. I just wanted to know if you'd like to go in to Houston for dinner and a concert tonight."

"I'm sorry, Paul. I have other plans." She didn't mean to glance back toward the kitchen and Ian, but she must have made things clear.

"I see," Paul said. "I'll call you tomorrow."

Ian scowled as she came back into the kitchen. "The competition?"

She blushed. "Paul and I are just good friends."

"But he is the one that you've been seeing?"

"What difference does it make? You've been back with Melanie. I had every right—"

Here they were arguing again. They had spent just over an hour together, and things were back to normal. "I haven't been back with Melanie," he countered. "I've been spending my evenings alone."

"No wonder you're in such a bad mood," she snapped.

"You could fix that easily enough," he said, eyes on her steadily as he spoke.

Sarah wasn't sure how she managed to wind up in his arms. His lips came down on hers, and it was as if a string had been stretched too tightly and finally snapped. Sarah was lost in the kiss.

Sarah tried to think rationally after Ian had, reluctantly, gone home. She must have been crazy to think that she could resist this man. She faced the fact that she loved him desperately.

Enough, she wondered, to give up her career if he asked? Not that he *had* asked. Ian had made it clear what his interests were, and they certainly didn't include marriage, at least at the moment.

And when he finally did decide to settle

down—and he was obviously in no hurry—he wanted a hausfrau who would bear him six or seven children. She wasn't sure she could manage six children, but three or four might be a possibility. She shoved her head under the pillow to try to blot out the thought. *She* wanted a liberated man—like Paul, came the errant thought—who would encourage her to rise to the top of her profession. What, then, was she doing with Ian?

Paul called on Sunday morning. Well timed, she thought; she was due to drive to Ian's in another hour, but she did feel that she owed Paul some sort of explanation—and she preferred to take care of that when Ian wasn't around.

"Are you busy tonight?" Paul asked hesitantly.

He seemed to be certain of what her answer would be. Sarah wondered just how much he had read in her eyes in that brief moment at the door of her apartment. "Yes, Paul," she said almost sadly, "I'm afraid I'm going to be tied up for some time to come."

"Your boss?"

"Yes," she admitted.

"It's none of my business, Sarah, even if it didn't sound like sour grapes . . . but isn't that a bad idea?"

"It's probably the stupidest thing I've ever done in my life!" she blurted out.

Paul laughed. "Well, since you recognize it, there's no point in my giving you any brotherly advice. We've been good friends—let's continue as that, in any case. And I've got a strong shoulder, if you discover that you need one to cry on."

Sarah's mind was on Paul as she dressed for her day with Ian. Why, she wondered, couldn't she feel about Paul the way she felt about Ian? Things would be far less complicated.

Ian kissed her tenderly as she arrived. "I love you, Sarah," he said, burying his face in her hair, and her heart soared at the long-awaited words.

They broke apart reluctantly and then, in a romantic glow, took off for a ride along the Gulf, stopping for a long lunch at a delightful restaurant. Afterward they drove along the Gulf again before Ian brought Sarah back to her condo. All in all it had been a joyous day—one they hated to end.

As Sarah mounted the ladder of the rig on Monday morning, she was certain that she heard muttered comments. She blushed at the thought of what the men might be saying and then pulled herself together. It was nonsense to assume that there could be any rumors already. Just because she felt that her happiness must be written all over her face. . . . She could hardly wait for the shift to be over so she could spend the evening with Ian.

Tuesday brought the first of the real problems with the drilling, though the problems were hardly unexpected. The drill bit was finally dull, and it had to be replaced. The engine was stopped, the couplings were unscrewed, and the drill pipe was pulled out of the hole. The string of pipe was raised to the top of the derrick, and then that section was unscrewed. The next section was raised and unscrewed, and yet another. Sarah held her breath.

Finally the new bit was in place and the operation was reversed. Mike Adams had probably done it hundreds of times; he was probably not sweating profusely as Sarah was. He was probably not worried about dropping something—a tool or a string of pipe—into the well, an accident that could, at best, hold them up for weeks, or, at worst, necessitate the abandonment of the well. Somehow Sarah knew that Ian's father—and some of the men, and maybe even Ian himself—would blame her for any such accident, even though her hands hadn't touched the tools or the controls.

Sarah was beginning to feel hopeful about the way things were going with Ian. They both enjoyed sailing and swimming, and walking along the deserted beach, looking at the marsh birds and the other wildlife. They enjoyed the same music and the same books. But much was missing—or unavailable. In a secret relationship it isn't possible to find out if two people like the same friends—or the same movies or plays or restaurants.

Their relationship was growing, but it still seemed, much to Sarah's distress, like a temporary thing. The future was never discussed. Sarah would have liked to argue about women's careers, about children—anything to bring their differences out into the open, where they could be looked at objectively. But she hesitated to be the one to change the level of what they were now enjoying.

On Monday she was certain that she wasn't imagining the snide comments on the rig. She tried to convince herself that her time spent with Ian had left her expecting the worst, but there were several looks and whispers that she couldn't ignore.

She went home at the end of that day and collapsed on her bed in tears, exhausted from the strain of pretending that she didn't hear or didn't care.

When Ian arrived to take her out to dinner, she launched into an attack. "The men know. They're whispering about us behind my back."

He rubbed his chin as he thought about it. "Hardly surprising, really. Do you think it's affecting anyone's work?"

His rig again! That was all that he ever thought of. "It's affecting *my* work," she said sharply.

"Then perhaps you should resign."

"You'd like that, wouldn't you!" Sarah's nerves had been on edge all day long, and Ian had managed to say exactly the wrong thing. "That's what you've wanted all along. That's probably the reason for this whole—for this whole—" Sarah couldn't continue. She collapsed on the sofa in tears, only barely aware of the slamming of the door as Ian walked out.

Sarah marched onto the rig on Tuesday with her head held high. She ignored the whispers, issuing her usual orders in a firm but friendly tone of voice. *So what?* she thought. *So what if they know, or think that they know, that I'm in love with Ian? In the long run they still have to judge me as an engineer, as their supervisor. None of them is stupid enough to conclude that I got this job because of how he feels about me.*

She tried to keep her mind on the job, but she kept remembering the evening before, when Ian had stormed out. She felt guilty about doubting his sincerity, but she had to consider the possibility that her words, flung at him in anger, had actually contained a germ of truth. If he wanted her off this rig, this just might work.

This was far more subtle than outright harassment. He knew that she wouldn't have hesitated to file another lawsuit if he had made dating him a condition of the job . . . or if he had taunted her in front of the men or refused to give her any responsibility. He had been so careful to avoid falling into any of those traps.

But this . . . this was clever. She could hardly file suit claiming that he had courted her so that she would crack under the strain of the crew's comments. And how did they find out so quickly, anyway? Melanie . . . Melanie was probably spreading the word. At Ian's suggestion?

Sarah was brought back to attention by a question from one of the crew. She answered it easily enough, but the incident left her shaken. A long-ago comment of Ian's came to mind: "An oil rig is a dangerous-enough place in any case. . . ." It was true that this stage, the early drilling, was boring, but that didn't mean that the supervisor could daydream.

Ian was waiting as she drove up to her apartment. He opened the car door for her and took her arm to help her alight. "I'm sorry about last night," he said as he walked with her to the elevator.

"I'd like a week off," Sarah said when they entered her apartment.

He raised an eyebrow. "Already? You've been working only a month."

Had it really been only a month? It seemed so much longer. "I wouldn't expect to be paid," she explained. "My old roommate is coming for a visit. We've booked a cruise to Mexico, but that's for the weekend, so that's no problem. I just thought . . . it's the week that you'll be coming back to the rig, anyway, so I really won't be needed. It would be nice to be able to spend my days with Barbara as well as my evenings."

"You'll be spending your evenings with *Barbara?*" he teased. "And what am I supposed to do? Run back to Melanie?"

Sarah blushed and wondered when she would ever be able to be as casual as he was about their relationship. *"If* I could spend some of the days with Barbara, I would feel less guilty about deserting her for an occasional evening!"

"Ah, the advantages of being the boss's girlfriend. Yes, Sarah, you may have that week off—without pay, of course. In fact, it solves another problem. You'd said that there is still some whispering going on among the men—

can you imagine what it will be like for us to be working together on that rig? Every time I look at you, they'll be watching and trying to interpret the expression on my face.

"We'll have to face that, of course; I doubt if the oil will come in during that week, and you can't continue on an unpaid leave indefinitely. Still, by the second week we should be getting close, and the well will be competing with us for their interest. Yes . . . by all means take the time off. That's what? Three weeks from now?"

Three weeks. It seemed an eternity. Sarah realized just how much she was being affected by the snide comments of the men. It seemed to be getting worse each day. She knew that she should be able to handle this—that it was a part of her job to manage to command the crew's respect.

She had been considering making a little speech, letting them know that she knew what they were saying and that it didn't bother her and that it had nothing to do with her work. But she knew also that that was childish. Surely the correct procedure was to ignore the whole thing. Eventually they would tire of their game. Eventually the oil would come in, and they would be too busy to indulge in senseless gossip.

She hadn't told Ian exactly how bad it was.

On many nights she had wanted to cry on his shoulder, but she was still trying to prove to him that she didn't need help with this job— not with any aspect of it.

There was another reason, though, for not sharing the problem with Ian—one that she tried to ignore but never quite succeeded. She was not entirely certain that Ian was innocent. The furtive thought that had crossed her mind now refused to leave—Ian could be encouraging the men to whisper behind her back. Ian could, even now, with all they were sharing, be trying to get her to quit.

Three weeks, she reminded herself as she climbed the ladder next morning and heard the whispers begin again. *Three weeks until Barbara comes and I can escape for a week. Some great job! I've been at it for a little over a month, and I'm already counting the days until my first vacation.*

She squared her shoulders and set her jaw. If the men were simply amusing themselves at her expense, they would stop sooner or later when they saw that it wasn't bothering her. And if Ian *was* behind all this . . . well, it would be a cold day in hell before she would let him force her to quit, before she would let him *win.*

It was another boring day. She could hardly wait to tell Barbara all about the excitement of field work. The first week had been exciting, because she was learning so much that was new—and, she had to admit, because she had been so fascinated by Ian. The day that the drilling had started had been exciting, too—for about half an hour. Changing the bit had been exciting. That would probably have to be done again soon. After that she was sure that there was one more exciting day yet to come—the day they struck oil. Aside from that, the whole thing had been a drag. It made her appreciate her old desk job, where there had been new challenges every day.

Lunchtime had been particularly bad today. She tried hard to join in the conversation and was convinced that she was being deliberately excluded. When would it stop? How many months would it take before she was accepted as one of the guys? Or had she done away with that possibility forever, now that she was the boss's girlfriend?

She debated, for the umpteenth time, whether or not to discuss the whole thing with Ian. If he really was not responsible, he might be able to offer some good advice. If he really was not responsible, he had a right to know what the problems were on his rig. If he really was not responsible . . . it always came back to that, to that same big *if.*

Barbara would be here soon. She would be able to discuss it with Barbara. That would be better anyway—an unbiased, outside opinion. She was so anxious for Barbara to come. . . .

"It's blowing!"

"Oil!"

"Strike!"

"Blowout!"

Sarah was shaken out of her musings by the shouts from the men. It couldn't be! It was too soon to strike oil. She looked in dismay at the shower of black gold that was raining down on them. "Cap it!" she screamed.

Chapter Eight

*M*IKE Adams was issuing hurried commands, commands that Sarah knew should be coming from her. She stood there in a state of shock as the sticky oil rained down on them. She watched in almost a detached way as the men rigged a pulley to the waiting "Christmas tree" that was to have topped the rig when they were closer to the oil. She mentally amended her thoughts—when they had *expected* to be closer to the oil. She ruefully admitted that there was no way to be closer than they were at the moment.

The Christmas tree was hoisted to the top of the rig, and Mike and another man scrambled up the derrick. She raised her head to watch, squinting to keep the black drops out of her eyes. Surely they would get it capped; surely they wouldn't stand here watching while millions of gallons of oil were lost.

She was interrupted by a tap on the shoulder. One of the older men stood next to her, shaking his head sadly. "I'd call the boss if I were you, ma'am," he said. "They might get it capped, or they might not, but Ian would want to know right away."

He was right, she knew. She had hoped . . . perhaps they would have it capped in a few minutes. Then she would have *good* news to report. The oil was in . . . and well before the building crew was finished with Number Two rig. There was no doubt now that this would be a fertile field. The building crew could go on to build the permanent station that she and Ian had discussed. She would be needed. With several rigs in operation, both she and Ian would be needed as supervisors.

She shook her head. The old man was still standing next to her. "I'll make the call for you if you like, ma'am," he said. "I don't blame you for hesitating. Ian isn't going to be very happy about this at all."

Sarah pulled herself together. It was her job, and she wasn't coping with it very well. "Thanks, anyway, Scottie," she said. "He may as well take it out on me." She turned to the station-to-shore telephone and took a deep breath.

Melanie answered the phone. "Is Ian there, please?" Sarah asked, trying to keep her voice from shaking.

"No, he's not." Sarah could almost hear the pleasure in the receptionist's voice as she made it clear that her boss wasn't available to talk to Sarah.

"Melanie, this is an emergency. Can you reach him?"

Something of Sarah's anguish must have been relayed over the phone; Melanie's tone changed to one of concern. "He's on Number Two rig, Sarah. I can call him from here. What's the problem?"

Sarah wanted to tell him herself, but that wasn't going to be possible. The two rigs each had a telephone connection back to the office, but not as yet to each other. Sarah would have to relay her bad news through Melanie. "A blowout," she said dully, looking up again to where Mike Adams and his assistant struggled against the force of the erupting well, trying to get the Christmas tree in place so that its many valves could be used to control the outflow of oil. "Mike and Sam are trying to cap it now."

Sarah stood on the platform, dejectedly looking up at the two men at the top of the rig, then off into space in the direction of Number Two rig. Ian should be arriving soon. The oil still rained down. Any hopes she might have had that it would soon be capped had long since disappeared. She wondered how many days it would take for the oil to reach the beaches. She couldn't help but think of the tanker spill in Valdez, Alaska, and the devastation it had wrought. The circumstances were quite different here, of course, but Sarah knew that a blowout could be just as harmful. She had seen pictures of the Texas beaches after the blowout of the big Mexican well. She remembered the dying marsh birds, their feathers too gummed up to allow them to fly or swim. Tears sprang to her eyes as she thought back to her walk with Ian along the unpolluted beach.

The launch was coming. Her knees felt wobbly as Ian's face came into focus, his jaw set firmly as he shaded his eyes to look up to the top of the rig. He scrambled up the ladder to the platform before his crewman had even secured the launch. He barely glanced at Sarah before he started climbing the rig.

Sarah watched in silence as he neared the top where Mike and Sam were still struggling against the force of the rushing oil. She muttered a silent prayer as Ian added his efforts to those of the other two men. Long minutes went by. "They're not going to do it," someone muttered. "They'll never get the Christmas tree on."

As if that were a signal for defeat, Sam turned to bellow down to the onlookers, "We can't manage the Christmas tree. Hoist up a temporary cap."

Sarah breathed a sigh of relief. Of course.

They tried the most sensible thing first, tried to get the Christmas tree in place so that the well could begin pumping through the complex valves directly into a tanker. But when that didn't work, they were resorting to their next line of attack—at least getting the well capped so that this horrible waste and pollution would stop. Afterward, she assumed, there would be a way to attach the Christmas tree, perhaps through some sort of check valve on the temporary cap. Her spirits brightened as she watched the huge metal cap make its journey up the pulley to the top of the rig.

"No chance," came a soft whisper that she was probably not meant to overhear. "Ain't seen such a big blow since '55, and they didn't get that one capped for ten days—not till they'd lost so much oil that the pressure had dropped nearly in half."

Ten days? Sarah felt a chill run through her. Ten days. Could it possibly rain oil for ten days? Billions of gallons of the precious black gold. Billions of dollars. All washed up on the beach. Sarah felt sick.

She turned to the men. "Can't anyone else help? We're all just standing here watching."

Someone looked at her scornfully, as if she had no idea of what might be involved. "Take a look, ma'am. There's barely room for the three of them at the top of the derrick. We'll help, all right, when the word comes to tear the derrick down to deck level. Then we'll pull ol' Sadie over to lend us some muscle power and see if we can get this sucker capped." The man gestured to a huge piece of equipment that Sarah dimly remembered was an emergency item. It looked as if it could slide a cap over an open wellhead and then screw it down into position. Her spirits gave another little surge of hope.

"How long . . . how long would it take to pull down the derrick?" she asked. She was sounding woefully inexperienced, but she didn't care. After all, this was an experience that most petroleum engineers hoped never to have. She wondered if it had ever happened to Ian before. He certainly seemed to know what he was doing.

"Day . . . maybe day and a half."

Sarah felt the shock of that casual comment. That long. The beaches would be ruined by then.

"And"—she was nearly afraid to ask—"once we're down to platform level, does ol' Sadie always come through?"

"Shucks, no, ma'am. In a blowout like this, it ain't certain that anything . . . or anybody can come through. If you ask me, this well's a dead loss. If he's lucky, she won't drain the whole field before he can get her capped."

That explained why no one had immediately given the order to rip down the derrick. If nothing was certain, if there was no sure way of getting it capped, Ian would be almost mentally tossing a coin to decide on his plan of attack. She turned her face upward again, shielding her eyes with her hand.

The temporary cap had reached the top, and the three men were struggling to get it into position. She could see their muscles bulging through their coveralls. She realized just how useless she was, standing here asking questions. She couldn't really even be of much help if Ian gave the order to tear down the derrick. Never had she been quite so aware of her lack of physical strength.

She could feel the tension among the crew as they watched the three men at the top. They were swinging a several-ton metal cap into position against the force of thousands of pounds of pressure. "Never seen anybody get it on the first try," someone said disconsolately.

She watched as the huge cap slipped and swung, still supported by the pulley that had hoisted it to the top. Ian jumped to the side, just as the cap smashed into the derrick where he had stood an instant before. For the first time Sarah realized what real danger the three at the top were in. She bit a knuckle and took a deep breath, trying to fight her rising nausea.

The men tried again to position the enormous cap. Again it swung away as it was buffeted by the force of the stream of oil. This time it was Mike who had to leap for his life. Sarah looked away as the burly man hung by one arm from the upper level of the derrick. The cap continued to swing like some gigantic pendulum. Ian timed its arc carefully, then ran to Mike and grabbed his free arm. Ian ducked as the cap passed over them again, then quickly straightened and pulled Mike up to the landing. They seemed to be conferring briefly; then all three men headed down the derrick as the cap continued to swing in an ever-decreasing arc.

"Are they giving up? Will we be tearing down the derrick now?" Sarah cursed her stupidity, but she needed to know what was going on.

"Hard to say, ma'am," one of the men replied, "but if I know the boss, he ain't ready to give up yet. I don't think he'll tear down the derrick until Billy Joe from the northern fields has had a go at it—and maybe the old man as well. I think they're just coming down now for safety harnesses. Those three know danged well that they should've put 'em on to start with, but it always takes a near accident like Mike just had to make 'em think of themselves when their minds 're on the well."

Not tear down the derrick until Billy Joe—whoever that was—had a go at it? How soon could this Billy Joe be here? And the old man? Who would that be? They were wasting time. No, maybe not—not if it would take over a day to pull down the derrick, anyway. It was a gamble, a gamble that Sarah wasn't certain she would have been prepared to take. She still had so much to learn—not only facts, but the instinctive feelings for which decisions to make in which emergencies.

Ian caught her eye as he reached the bottom of the derrick. "Sarah," he said sharply, "take the launch back to Number Two rig. They'll want to know the situation."

She opened her mouth to protest. "I could call Melanie to report, and she could call them."

His eyes hardened. "Sarah, that was an order. There's plenty for you to do there, and you'll be good for nothing here, anyway. They're probably all sitting on their hands waiting for some word. Get them back to work. If we lose this well, it will be more important than ever to bring that one in."

Sarah's eyes smarted. She didn't have to be reminded of how useless she was in this situation. She headed to the launch. Ian called to her, and she turned to meet his cold eyes. "Call Melanie from there, will you? Tell her to contact Billy Joe and the old man. I want them here right away."

Ian was right, as usual, Sarah admitted as she approached the launch. The crew stood about listlessly, obviously worried and waiting for word from Number One rig. The men seemed happy to see Sarah, and, to her, they seemed at this point like old friends. She interrupted their rush of questions. "Just a minute, men. Ian asked me to telephone a message to the office first. Then I'll tell you whatever I can. Briefly, though—no, it's not capped yet."

She relayed her message calmly to Melanie. When Melanie responded with, "It was a blow-out, then?" Sarah realized that she had never given the other woman any real information in the first place. Feeling somewhat guilty, she bit her tongue to keep from snapping that Ian would provide the details. She offered the same information that she had just given the building crew—that the blowout had not yet been capped.

"I guessed that, if he wants Billy Joe and the old man," Melanie replied tartly.

Sarah was sorry that she'd bothered to attempt any explanations. She hung up to face the men.

"There's nothing to say," the crew foreman said. "We heard you say that he wants Billy

Joe and the old man. That pretty much says it all. He's going to attempt to get it capped without tearing down the derrick, then. Well, those two have managed it before."

Sarah looked at him helplessly. "Everyone knows more about it than I do," she admitted. "There was nothing that I could tell you, but what can you tell me? What are the odds— either way? Who is the old man? How often has this happened to Ian before?"

One of the older crew members stepped forward. Like most of the men his age, he had seemed opposed to Sarah from the beginning. But now his eyes were kind. "Admitting what you don't know is the first step to learning a lot, lassie," he said. "No one here expects you to know everything that those of us who have been with the old man from the beginning know. I've been with him since '45, and I've seen four wells blow. The old man and Billy Joe got all of 'em capped, without tearing down the derricks. 'Course, this time they'll likely tear down the derrick, anyway, while they're waiting for the old man. It's sure to take him a couple of days to get here."

"Where is he?" It seemed to Sarah that a private plane could bring someone from the northern part of the state in a couple of hours.

"Hasn't Ian mentioned? He's in Scotland,

helping with the bringing in of the North Sea oil."

Ian's father! The old man they'd all been talking about was Ian's father, who was convinced that women on a rig were bad luck. Well, this was certainly not going to do anything to change his mind—or Ian's, for that matter.

"And Billy Joe? Where is he?"

"He's at the big MacDonald field, ma'am. They should get him here by tonight. Likely he and Ian will have a try at capping her with the derrick in place, but by tomorrow morning I think they'll pull the derrick."

Sarah mulled over what she'd learned. She turned to the men and smiled. "Ian told me to get you guys back to work," she said. Then her eyes grew sober. "He says that Number Two rig is more important than ever now."

It was a quiet afternoon. The men worked hard, as if they were anxious to turn their attention to something useful. Sarah hoped for a phone call from Melanie telling her that the well had been capped, but the phone stayed maddeningly silent. Sarah watched the men and made suggestions as she noted how things were going, but her mind was on Number One rig with Ian. Was he still risking his life at the top of the derrick? She knew that the men were thinking much the same thoughts as she; there was none of the usual banter among the workers.

The hours dragged by. At four o'clock the men straggled to the launch, except for the two who were staying for a double shift to provide nighttime security. They would return in the small boat brought out by their relief at midnight.

The men were as silent on the return ship as they had been during the day. Sarah found herself looking down into the water, searching for traces of the gooey oil that would all too soon be washing in toward shore.

She stood on the dock after disembarking, looking out to sea instead of heading to her car. One of the crew members stopped and looked at her searchingly. "It's been a busy day, Sarah," he said. "You should go home and get some rest."

"I thought I'd wait here for the crew from Number One," she replied.

"No point," he answered. "They'll stay the night. They'll want to be there when Billy Joe arrives, and they'll get right to work pulling down the derrick if he has no more luck than Ian and Mike. You'll not see any of them till the well's capped—or blown up, whichever comes first."

"Blown up?" A new concern showed on Sarah's grimy face.

"Aye," he replied. "Could happen accidentally, if a storm hits. Lot of oil out there, just waiting for a spark or a flash of lightning. But they could blow it on purpose, too, if they can't get it capped. Usually plugs it up just fine. It would at least prevent this blow from depleting the whole field, though of course it would be the end of Number One well."

Sarah felt sick again. It hadn't occurred to her that this well might not be salvageable or that the whole field could be lost. There was so much she had to learn. She wiped a hand across her oil-streaked face. For the first time that day she gave some thought to her own position as she realized that Ian might not give her a chance to learn anything else—might not want her back on his rig at all.

Her lack of knowledge hadn't caused the blowout—more experienced petroleum engineers than she had made the original prediction of how far down the oil was expected to be. And her lack of knowledge hadn't made things any worse after the accident occurred. Mike Adams, as Ian originally had assured her, knew exactly what to do in any event. And Ian had been there within half an hour, not that his presence had made any real difference, either.

No, there was no way that either she or Ian could possibly feel that the fault lay with

Sarah. But that was being rational, and the MacDonalds had never been rational about having Sarah on the rig. Even if, by some miracle, Ian were on her side, there was still the "old man," the owner of MacDonald Oil. A woman was a jinx, the old man had said, and he would certainly feel that he had been proved right.

The crew member was still standing next to her, looking at her with some concern. "Sarah?" he repeated. "You'd really better get some rest. You told us yourself that we've got to concentrate on Number Two rig—and you'll be part of our team again while Ian's on Number One."

Part of our team again. Sarah managed a small smile in appreciation. It was nice to know that she'd been accepted, now that it was probably too late. She waved good-bye tiredly and headed to her car.

"Take off your coveralls before you get in the car," he called after her. "You'll never get the stains off the seats otherwise." She looked down, for the first time, at her oil-soaked coveralls. She held out her hands for inspection, hardly believing that she hadn't really noticed them until now.

She walked to the car and glanced into the side view mirror. She looked as if she were in blackface for one of those old-time minstrel shows. She stepped out of her grimy coveralls, rolled them into a ball, and stashed them in the car trunk. She wiped her hands hard along the sides of her jeans, not even wanting to touch the steering wheel until the worst of it was off. The hard hat she left on. Under it, she hoped, her hair had escaped most of the black rain.

She laughed to herself as she turned the key in the ignition, as the image of the girl in the commercial came back to her. Tonight Sarah was definitely in no shape to shake out her hair and go right to the nearest disco.

"I'll call Melanie as soon as we get out to the rig," Sarah promised her crew in the morning. "Maybe there will be good news. Maybe Billy Joe arrived and they got it capped last night."

"I don't think so, Sarah," one of the men said, his face somber. "If they'd capped it, I think Ian would've called you—even in the middle of the night. He'd know that you'd want to know."

If he even cares now, she thought. Somehow she knew that she couldn't compete with the rig. Not that she'd meant it to be a contest, but if he felt that in some way it had been her fault. . . . "He'd know that you'd want to know, too," she answered, "but they could have been near dead with exhaustion by then.

He'd know that I'd call the office this morning, anyway."

Melanie brought Sarah up to date in a rather toneless voice. She sounded tired. Sarah wondered if she had been at her desk all night waiting for word. There was, in fact, not much news. Billy Joe had arrived by eight, and he, Ian, and Mike had tried for several hours to cap the erupting well. The rest of the crew had been sent home at the end of their usual shift to catch a few hours' sleep, since they wouldn't be useful until the decision was made to pull down the derrick.

By midnight, in exhaustion and exasperation, Ian and Billy Joe had given up. The derrick would come down when the crew arrived back on board this morning. The "old man," Ian's father, was due in late this evening. By tomorrow morning he would be on hand when they tried to cap the well at platform level.

Sarah gave her report to the men, and they plunged into work as if it would take their minds off the scene that was being enacted just a few miles away. Sarah was happy to be at work, too, here with the building crew who had seemingly accepted her, here where she knew the routine and felt that she was contributing in some way.

She wondered if Ian would appear on the scene. He, like herself, couldn't really be useful on Number One today. There was nothing that could be done now until the rigging was dismantled. She couldn't believe that he would have been able to sleep for more than a few hours. Either he was standing out in that rain of oil on Number One, lending moral support to the men who were tearing down the derrick, or he would show up here.

It was midafternoon when she heard the small boat approaching. Ian had obviously spent some of the day on Number One, because he was as oil-covered as she had been the day before. The men gathered around as he reached the top of the ladder.

He avoided looking at Sarah. "No news, men, as I guess you know," he said, his jaw clenched as if in pain. "But the old man will be here tonight, sooner than I had dared to hope. So I've decided to wait for him before deciding whether or not to tear down the derrick. If he says the word, we'll spend tonight and tomorrow pulling it down and get it capped by tomorrow night." He tried for a smile. "A platform-level cap will be a piece of cake for the old man."

He looked coldly at Sarah. "You can take the boat back to shore. I'll take the rest of this shift. There's nothing I can do on Number One."

Sarah opened her mouth to protest. He was

making it clear already that he wanted her out of the way. She looked at him with grief-stricken eyes, meeting his steely ones. He looked exhausted. She started to tell him that he needed more rest, that she was perfectly capable of directing this crew. Then she realized that he was doing what he needed to be doing. Taking this shift would keep him busy, would keep his mind off the debacle on Number One, about which he could do nothing until morning.

She lifted her chin. "All right, Ian," she said. "I'll take over here again tomorrow, while you're trying to cap the well."

She climbed down the ladder and into the small boat. She pulled the cord twice before the motor caught, then headed toward shore without looking back. He probably would neither notice nor care, but she still didn't want him to see the tears in her eyes.

Chapter Nine

*S*ARAH was relieved to find Paul at home. She tried for a small smile when he came to the door. "Is that shoulder still available?" she asked.

He held her while she cried and then set her to work fixing a salad. She knew that he was trying to keep her too busy to think, but tearing the lettuce didn't really take any mental effort. "The beaches—" she began, and burst into tears again.

"There will be volunteers," he replied calmly. "There always are. Some marsh birds will die, but we'll save most of them. It won't be another Alaska. You'll see."

She tried to blink back the tears. "I'll be fired."

"Sarah, you have a three-year contract. You can't be fired for something that was in no way your fault."

"Then they'll make my life so miserable that I'll have no choice. I'll have to quit."

"Don't jump to conclusions, Sarah. Play it by ear. There are no decisions that have to be made tonight . . . or even tomorrow. C'mon now—set the table."

Eventually she had no more tears. Paul walked her to her door and kissed her on the tip of the nose. She wished once again that she could fall in love with this man.

Sarah expected to toss and turn all night, but exhaustion won out. She was asleep within minutes.

The phone awakened her. A glance in the direction of the open shutter revealed the gray sky that precedes the dawn. She reached groggily for the phone.

There was no mistaking the voice, though he sounded near dead with fatigue. "We capped it," he said. There was none of the enthusiasm that should have accompanied that announcement, just the flat, leaden statement. "We got it about an hour ago—way past the time when we should have given up, but neither Dad nor I really wanted to give the order to pull down the derrick. We got it. The temporary is on. We'll give it a day or two to settle down, and then we'll get the Christmas tree up." A bit of excitement crept into his voice, cutting through the exhaustion. "We did it, Sarah. We capped it."

She hardly knew what to say. "It's a miracle," she whispered.

"No, just the years of experience of Billy Joe

and the old man. That and the MacDonald luck." She could almost hear the grin now. "Anyway, Sarah, I'd like you on Number Two today. I'll call you this evening and fill in some details. Right now I've got to get some sleep."

Sarah was certainly fully awake. The well was capped, and he wanted her back on Number Two. She wasn't sure which was the greater miracle. She'd been certain that she'd never set foot on one of his rigs again.

When Ian called that evening, she realized that she'd been too hasty in believing in miracles. His call was terse and to the point: The old man was insisting that Sarah be reassigned. No, she wasn't fired, but the old man wanted her off the rig. She could work in the office, trying once again to make a dent in that paperwork.

Sarah protested, thinking of days spent alone with Melanie. "The men on Number Two were great today, Ian. They accept me— I know they do. They're not blaming me for the blowout—"

He interrupted. "It's not going to be decided by polling the men, Sarah. This isn't a democracy. It's a company, and the old man happens to own it. If he wants you off the rig, you're off the rig. He said that the next female on a MacDonald rig will have to step over his dead body to get there. Besides, he'll be taking over

Number One for a few days, and so I'll be on Number Two."

It was futile to argue. Sarah consoled herself with the thought that Barbara would arrive in two weeks. Surely she could still have her unpaid vacation—in fact, the old man would probably like to make it permanent.

The oil found its way to the beaches in exactly a week. Ian called to suggest that she join the volunteers who would be scrubbing each oil-fouled bird. She didn't even bristle when he mentioned that it would be good public relations. She recognized, even through her disappointment and anger, that saving the birds meant more to Ian than just good PR.

Despite her apprehensions she and Melanie had been working well together. She'd made a big dent in the backlog of paperwork. She was enjoying being behind a desk again. Still, she welcomed the opportunity to join the volunteers on the beaches.

Nothing had quite prepared her for her first look at the mess created by the oil. She wanted to just sit down and cry, but she forced herself to approach a group that seemed to know what needed to be done. She spent several hours cleaning up sticky seabirds and "testing" them in small ponds built by the volunteers for that purpose, to see if the birds had lost too much of the natural oils that allow them to stay afloat.

She spent a few more hours scooping up and bagging the absorbent granules that had been spread over the water surface by MacDonald soon after the blowout occurred. This new material had collected much of the spill, but the birds still managed to find their way into the goop.

She looked up as the sun was setting to find Ian standing a few paces away. He walked over and squatted down beside her. "Have we lost many, do you think?" he asked.

"I haven't seen any dead ones yet," she replied carefully. "Will the ones that we clean up all be okay?"

"I think so." He stood up and reached down to take her hand. As he pulled her to her feet, she realized just how tired and stiff she was.

"How about some dinner?" he asked.

Sarah thought about it carefully and shook her head. She had too many things to sort out in her own mind. She bit her lip as she watched him walk away.

Ian's father stayed on. Sarah saw nothing of Ian. She spent a whole week helping with the beach-cleaning effort. Paul joined them for three days when he was on night duty. She spent evenings with him when she could and counted the days until Barbara arrived. She continued to beat her way through the accumulated paperwork. She would almost have been enjoying herself, enjoying the feeling of accomplishment, except that she had a point to prove. She knew that the men had accepted her, and she wanted back on that rig.

Barbara would understand, she told herself as she drove to Houston to meet her old roommate's plane.

They talked nonstop for the two and a half hours that it took to drive back to Galveston and had barely begun to catch up on their three months apart. Sarah realized more than ever how much she had missed this friend. They sat on the deck before dinner, sipping tall drinks. The remaining traces of oil that still dotted the beach were not visible at this distance, especially in the dwindling light. Barbara sighed contentedly, and Sarah got up to start cooking.

The doorbell rang. Paul handed Sarah a bottle of wine. "No, I won't come in," he replied to her invitation. "I know that you two have lots to talk about. But if you begin to get sore throats from talking so much, come and see Dr. Paul. I'll prescribe some dancing in the party room."

Sarah grabbed his hand and dragged him through her apartment and out to the deck as he continued to protest that he didn't want to intrude. She introduced him to Barbara, pushed him down in her vacated chair, and went to get him a drink. "Stay," she insisted. "Keep Barbara company while I fix dinner. The kitchen is really too small for more than one person."

She assembled a casserole and put it into the oven, then fixed the salad. She returned to the deck to find that her two dearest friends were well on their way to becoming dear friends— the electricity that surged between them was what she wished that she had found with Paul instead of with Ian. She stifled a grin and insisted that Paul stay for dinner.

Sarah was happy that she had arranged to take a week off so that she could have the days to spend with her friend, because Barbara spent most of her evenings with Paul. They always made an effort to include her, and she did join them for dinner most evenings. She knew that they didn't feel that she was intruding, and yet she was well aware that they had discovered something special and that they needed time alone to find out just how special it really was.

With only a small twinge of regret, she pressured Paul into taking her place on the weekend cruise to Mexico. She waved adieu to her starry-eyed friends and went home to soak in the condo's hot tub. She was happy for Barbara and Paul. She was almost beginning to hope, even though it was clearly too soon, that this relationship would be important enough to lure Barbara to Galveston.

Saturday. She was supposed to be enjoying a cruise. She got up early to walk the beach and soon found herself helping a group who were trying to remove the last of the oil. Scooping and sifting was a pleasant, mindless activity, and she actually forgot all of her woes for a little while.

She was enjoying the hot sun and the sea breeze when a shadow fell across the sand. She looked up to find Ian standing there.

"I thought this was the weekend of the cruise," he said.

"It is." She smiled ruefully. "I'm playing Cupid."

He reached for her hand and pulled her to her feet. They strolled along the water's edge, neither knowing what to say. "Melanie tells me that the mountain of papers is now just a small hill," he said tentatively.

She smiled. "Melanie tells me that the derrick is nearly done on Number Two," she countered.

He turned her to face him. "Do you think we could get back to talking to each other directly, instead of passing our messages through

Melanie?" Sarah lowered her eyes. He lifted her chin and forced her to meet his gaze. "Still mad at me?" he asked.

She nodded and then found her voice. "Ian, you took me off that rig. You know that I can't be blamed for the blowout, and yet you took me off the rig. I know that your father owns the company, but you're the president. That decision should have been yours—probably *was* yours. You went along with his silly superstitious nonsense. You're just as bad as he is. Of all the stupid, chauvinistic—"

"You're right." She looked at him in surprise, and he continued. "You're right, Sarah. My old man is an old fool. Even some of his old buddies have been telling him that. And you and I are going to go tell him that right now."

Sarah barely had time to take in what he had said. He led her to the pickup truck and helped her in. She was quiet as they drove to Ian's house. She was about to meet Ian's father, the owner of the company, and she was supposed to tell him that he was an old fool. Well, she thought, he *was* an old fool—and perhaps he needed to be told.

"Hey, you old fool," Ian yelled as he opened the front door. "Come and meet Sarah!"

An older version of Ian came in from the

deck. "So this is our bad-luck charm," he bellowed.

Sarah searched his face, certain that she saw the same glimmer of a smile that she knew so well in Ian.

"Hired by the *young* fool, weren't you?" He shot a baleful glance at Ian. "Young fool knows that women don't belong on an oil rig. Any fool knows that."

Ian grinned. "Don't weaken, Dad. I'd like to keep her in the office."

Sarah bristled. "If you two are done having your fun, I'd like to go home, Ian."

He grew more serious and turned to his father. "I wanted you to meet Sarah, Dad, but I also wanted to talk to you. We hired Sarah for a field position. That's what she wanted, and that's what we offered her. You *know* that you're being an old fool. Sarah's presence on that rig didn't cause the blowout. We've had them before, and we'll have them again.

"There's not a single man on that rig who blames Sarah. I know, because I've been talking to them. Some of them were against her at first, but she won them over. They want her back, Dad. They want to prove to her that they're behind her. I assume that you're going back to Scotland anyway. Let me handle this my way."

Ian's father had been trying to interrupt. He

spluttered, turned an amazing shade of blue, and fell to the floor. Sarah reached the phone before Ian could even react. She dialed 911 and described the symptoms and then ran back to see what could be done. Ian had already loosened his father's collar. He was conscious, and his color seemed to be improving. "Don't try to talk," Ian whispered. "The ambulance is on its way."

Ian and Sarah paced in the hospital waiting room. "Maybe I *am* bad luck," she suggested. "First the blowout, and now this."

He silenced her with a gentle kiss.

The young doctor appeared before too long. "It was a mild stroke, Mr. MacDonald. We'll keep him overnight, but I have no reason to think that we'll see a repeat. I can't find any permanent damage. You can see him now."

"Wait for me, Sarah," Ian said. "I won't stay long. He'll need some rest."

Ian was expecting a subdued, sick version of his father and was taken aback to find him sitting up in bed looking as fit as ever. "Bring the lass in here," he bellowed.

"That's not a good idea, Dad," Ian ventured. "I'm sure that you shouldn't be getting upset. It was our argument that brought this on in the first place."

"If you don't want me to get upset, you'll humor me. Now get her."

Sarah also thought it was a bad idea, but she agreed to see the elder Mr. MacDonald for a minute or two. "Well, lass," he chortled as she entered his room, "you've won. You're back on Number Two—since clearly I can't be." She tried to protest, but he interrupted. "Be quiet, the both of you. I'm the boss, and don't you forget it. Ian will be on Number One, Sarah will take Number Two, and I'll run the office until we find that business manager—as soon as they let me out of here."

She had won. There was no elation in the victory.

As the weeks went by, life settled back into some sort of routine. Sarah felt comfortable on Number Two rig, as the sequence of steps unfolded much as they had earlier on Number One. Ian was making plans for a permanent station out in the area that they had mapped earlier in the submersible; his geologists were now convinced that MacDonald owned a small but fertile field that would support several wells. Ian's father was feeling fit and anxious to be out of the office. As soon as they found a business manager, the old man would be back on a rig; Sarah would supervise the construction crew on the permanent station.

Sarah ate dinner with Paul about once a

week and smiled to herself as he rambled on about Barbara. He was planning a trip to New York when he finished this year of residency. He was staying in Galveston for at least one more year, but it was clear that this trip to New York would involve some discussion of whether Barbara might consider relocating. Sarah was so pleased to have brought these two together. If only she were able to do so well for herself!

She was certain that Ian was back to seeing Melanie. He was friendly enough, but he seemed to have decided that he was going to think of her as a wonderful engineer—period. At least his father now agreed.

The drilling, under Ian's supervision, began on Number Two. Sarah and the construction crew, who now seemed like old friends, moved on to begin the permanent platform. Ian's father took over Number One, joking that even an old sick man could keep an eye on that one now that it was running so smoothly.

A peaceful month went by, and then Sarah was surprised by a rig-to-rig phone call—over their newly installed system—from Ian. "Oil's in on Number Two," he announced gleefully. "Dad and I are going out to celebrate. We want you to join us."

Sarah thought back to the old TV commer-

cial as she drove home. She took off her hard
hat and shook out her hair. She stripped off her
coveralls and headed for the shower. Tonight
she did feel like that long-ago girl in the commercial, the one who was ready to metamor-
phose into a picture of feminity, ready for a
night of celebration.

She dressed carefully. It was a business dinner of a sort, but also a special occasion. She
chose a silky black dress with long sleeves,
puffed a little at the shoulders. A single strand
of pearls followed the line of the deep V neck-
line. Black strappy heels completed the outfit.
Her hair hung long and loose, shiny from the
shower. She noticed Ian's swift intake of breath
as she answered the door.

There was also an approving glance from his
father. She had thought that Melanie might be
along, but these two attentive escorts were hers
alone.

Ian's father ordered champagne and toasted
first Number Two, then Number One, then the
success of the whole operation. And then he
turned to Ian. "Well?" he asked. Ian shook his
head. "You're a fool," he said. "A young fool."

Sarah looked puzzled. She raised an inquir-
ing eyebrow at Ian. "We'd better dance," he
said, "or he'll take over this conversation entirely." He gave his father a withering look as
he led Sarah out to the dance floor. He then

maneuvered her skillfully out onto the balcony that overlooked the Gulf. The frothy whitecaps looked luminous in the moonlight.

"He wanted to know if I'd asked you to marry me," he said calmly, looking deep into her eyes.

Sarah couldn't believe that she'd heard him correctly. Her mind was racing. She knew that she loved him . . . at one point she'd even had some hope that he might love her. But for the past few weeks they'd seemed just like business associates. "Is this some new way to get me off the rig?" she asked.

"Only when the first child comes," he answered with a teasing smile. "Unless you'd rather have the office."

"Ian—"

His face grew serious. "Wait. I'm doing this badly. How many children we have will be up to you—just as whether you work on the rig, children or no children, will be your choice. You should know that by now. You know that I love you."

"I don't know that at all."

He took her into his arms and kissed her in a way that left her shaken. "I've loved you almost from the beginning, Sarah. Somehow the rig kept getting in the way. The old man has been giving me a hard time . . . he knows how

I feel about you and he was afraid I was going to let you slip away."

"Does your father make all your decisions for you?"

He refused to get angry at her. "Dad and I are both pretty stubborn, but neither of us is ever too stubborn to admit that the other may be right. I'm not going to let you go just *because* he's in favor of our marriage." He kissed her again. "Say yes, Sarah. Make my dad happy."

"Yes," she whispered and melted back into his arms.